About the Author

Dixy Gandhi is a mechanical engineer working in the corporate world. She describes herself as an introvert who has cloaked her shyness under arrogance and sometimes wears her cloak inside out. She explores coming-of-age themes, mental health, and relationships through her writings.

Mr. King of Spades

Dixy Gandhi

Mr. King of Spades

Olympia Publishers

London

www.olympiapublishers.com
OLYMPIA PAPERBACK EDITION

A CIP catalogue record for this title is
available from the British Library.

ISBN: 978-1-80439-585-1

This is a work of fiction.
Names, characters, places and incidents originate from the writer's
imagination. Any resemblance to actual persons, living or dead, is
purely coincidental.

First Published in 2024

Olympia Publishers
Tallis House
2 Tallis Street
London
EC4Y 0AB

Printed in Great Britain

Dedication

"Picasso would not be Picasso if he stopped painting just like that, you have to find yourself." Someone said those words and they inspire me to write and keep writing every day, even when life throws a curveball, when days get too long or when things seem out of control. For the love of words and the love of writing…

Acknowledgements

This book would not be complete without the encouragement of few people. Firstly, my mother for encouraging me in my every endeavor. My husband, Namdev, for not reading a word I wrote ever, but spending all long drives asking me for narrations of my stories and providing feedback. My friend, Ragini, for reading all the rewrites, and my selected close group of friends who always read every word I write.

Chapter 1

Platonic

I stood in front of the mirror, staring blankly into the eyes of the stranger looking back at me.

And then I blinked, with the blink, I was taken back to the day of my wedding, all decked up — standing in front of the huge mirror in the resort, with a maroon turban adorned with pearls on my head and a sword in my hand.

And all I wanted to do was run away. It wasn't a case of cold feet, I wanted to run away with the woman who was to be my bride, without the *shor-sharaba,* just the both of us. It's just a few hours, then we have our lives ahead of us, I reminded myself.

My reverie was broken with the notification from my Intel Pentium 4 Windows 98 PC shining on my face as I turned. I sat down in front of my CRT monitor and opened the notification.

I will join you in ten mins. Hungry, it read.

I clicked on one of the many windows open on my PC and started playing solitaire, no to be precise, I was playing Spider Solitaire with all the four suits and trust me, this is the most complicated part of the story.

Solving this puzzle.

The rest is simple. And also trust me as and when we end, we would wind up all packs in neat stacks, which would be the end of the game or the start of a new one? We will see.

The dogs were barking outside at a lone car on the road wondering how someone dared to claim their road at this time of the night. The numbers on the right corner of my screen said two fourty and I was wide awake, clicking to put cards in order, with only the light of the PC in the room and also waiting. I also had WinRAR open with the music blaring on my headphones. I clicked the arrow to right to skip to next song as the software shuffled to another folder and *Desert rain* music started playing.

And then I was back to Spider Solitaire.

But then the song was interrupted with the alert I was waiting for even as the Gtalk window at the right corner popped up with

U there?

I clicked on it immediately and typed, *Yes.*

So where was I? she wrote.

You had gone to grab a bite.

Yes. But what were we talking about? she typed next.

Scroll up, I typed.

You need a better attitude, she typed

I know, hearing that for the past twenty years.

It's because of your outdated PC. Update it and your attitude will upgrade too, she typed and ended with a smile emoji.

Update or upgrade? I typed.

What's the difference? she typed.

This is the reason we chat in this window and not use voice chat. Your language needs improvement. I am the only hope you have. Thereby eliminating the need for upgradation, I typed as fast as my fingers allowed.

I got a smile in return.

Go to sleep. We will talk tomorrow. It's late, she typed.

Okay. Will pick you up after office.

Like always, she typed and then a window said she was offline.

I continued playing Spider Solitaire.

When my eyes couldn't take it anymore, I logged off and went to bed with her thoughts on my mind.

Do I need a name for her? Or can I tell our story with the pronouns alone.

I think it's simple when someone is just a pronoun in your life. Like when you mention her, you know you mean her. I use it all the times.

When friends ask me if I am free for a movie in the evening. I say, 'No, I have plans.'

They give me a look and I shrug. 'It's her.'

And they know.

The very next step to this declaration is the urge of human mind to label our relationship. I run into many people who keep doing that, based on their experiences and their perspectives. So, I often hear, 'oh it's her' with the teasing elongation of the word 'her'. Sometimes colleagues say she is using me. I ignore such provocations.

I have a simple philosophy in life. When it comes to understanding the relationship two people share, it is best left to those two. No one else can judge them. No one else is equipped enough.

So, for me it's just her.

I don't need to explain anything to anyone. What I need though is to tell this story. As you must have guessed by now, I am a lover of the words.

One might think I am making it all about her. Maybe I am hopelessly in love with her. Maybe I am and I don't know.

I told you I plan to make it as simple as possible. So, let's get this aspect out of the way as well.

I lie on my bed and SMS her to get her side of the story.

Do you love me?

As I said let's remove all possible plot twists away. This may not be the smartest way to tell a story but I believe I need to be honest, not lead you on.

Go to sleep, Palash, she replied back.

I need an answer, I SMS again.

If we are post-apocalypse and the whole burden of repopulating the earth is on us. I would still say no, her SMS said.

See, that's what's called platonic. Not many people get it. But I know her. She is not into me. Nor am I.

We are just we.

Chapter 2

I am the King

Do you want to learn salsa?

I woke up to the sound of my mobile vibrating with her text. The mobile clock showed eight a.m.

Negative, I typed back sleepily and went back to bed.

When I checked my mobile again on the way to work some hours later there were few more from her.

Zumba?

Bollywood?

I kept scrolling down.

If only I could convince you to buy a smartphone. I would have sent you amazing links, her last text read.

Not interested in any dance form. Two left feet, I typed and hit send.

Within microseconds I got her reply.

K

A single letter — that coming from her meant she was giving up on the topic.

I sighed as I typed again. *What's the deal?*

Call, her reply said, which meant she was too bored to type. I dialed her number as I walked in my office.

"Hmm," I said as a means for her to go on and she launched into her explanation in fast hurried words where one word rolled into another, the way she always spoke.

"I am bored in the evenings. Might as well learn something new. But will be uncomfortable going alone. So thought you might be interested in joining them with me," she finished and waited for me to respond.

"We are together most of the evenings. And that bores you?" I asked calmly.

"No not you. The nothingness of evenings bores me."

"Okay. Join a class. Find a friend. I am not the one," I concluded.

She didn't argue.

"See you in evening then," she said

"Not today, lest you are bored," I replied and disconnected. I wasn't acting up.

This was us.

As I reached my cabin and switched on the work laptop, my mobile buzzed again.

You are no fun.

I know.

There was no further communication till lunch time, and I continued working. By lunch I had an email from her with attachments of couples in different poses with the labels of different dance forms. I scrolled down to bottom where she had typed *are you in?*

Still no, I replied.

Meet me in the evening.

Only if you promise you won't drag me to some stupid dance class.

She sent me a gif of a girl crossing her heart.

I was all about the words. She was all about the expressions and animations.

That made us perfect.

16

By eight p.m. I was parked outside her office, waiting patiently for her to come down.

"Why didn't you message that you are here?" she exclaimed as she hopped behind me.

"You will come when you are ready."

"See this is what I mean by nothingness. You act as if there is no other thing you would rather do than wait. You could have messaged me and I would have come down faster. But you chose to wait doing nothing."

"You did come when you could, right?" I questioned and she sighed.

"I don't understand you," she said and we rode in silence for a long time.

She still looked disturbed when we got down at a restaurant for dinner.

"What is it?" I asked.

"Nothing," she said and walked ahead of me.

I called after her and placed my arms around her shoulder as I explained, "When I chose to meet you in the evening, it means that I chose to spend time with you. Then it doesn't matter if you come now or an hour later. There's no other place I would rather be."

I shrugged. "What's the hurry?" I left it open for her to answer. That brought a smile to her face.

"That reminds me, what was the message last night, asking me if I loved you?" she counter questioned.

"Nothing. Was just sorting my thoughts."

"Do you?" she asked next as we seated opposite each other.

"Not there yet." I winked at her.

"What do you mean by not there yet?" She playfully hit me with the napkin. "You mean you intend to in future?"

17

"No, but just saying no to do you love me, sounded rude so I said not there yet."

"Then why ask me?" She was exasperated and I shrugged again.

"To keep it simple," I replied.

"You aren't that good looking or that interesting you know." She continued the banter.

"Define that?" I asked as I glanced through the menu in spite of knowing what I was going to order.

She looked confused.

"You said, that good looking, that interesting, what is the bar I am compared against?" I asked.

"I don't know. Howard Roark, Heathcliff…" She went on naming fictional characters. "Dean Winchester maybe."

"None of whom are real," I reminded her.

"But they are interesting nevertheless. Every single girl's dream."

I cleared my throat at that.

"What?" she asked.

"Except you aren't single," I reminded her and she bit her tongue.

"I know," she said, "too bad I keep forgetting about him."

"How is he, by the way?"

"Alive," she replied, munching on her nachos.

"I don't know, Palash. We haven't talked in weeks. The time difference and his busy schedule. It's simpler to forget about him."

"I doubt he feels the same," I replied.

"Maybe he does," she replied between bites. "Maybe he is cheating on me with someone out there, and then I would be free."

I kept observing her as she kept eating from all around the table, nachos then a sip of her Mocktail, then a bite of Indian food from my plate, again a sip of my coke.

"Break up then. If you are that unhappy," I remarked.

She winced at that.

"Except I am not. I really do love him. And if someone breaks up it would be him with me. Not vice versa," she announced and I was thrown back to the reverie of the time when he had proposed her.

Like I said, this story can only be told backwards.

She had acted like a teenager.

"What do I do?" she had asked me and I had no answer.

It was a time when we weren't intertwined like now. I was jealous. Not about someone proposing to her but her finding someone before me. Not that there was a competition, except that it was, then.

"Follow what your heart says," I had advised.

"I don't trust it anymore," she had replied. "I don't want to be the one to hurt anyone again."

"You won't," I had assured her.

And she had gone ahead and said yes. A week later he had left for States on business.

This was a year back, he visited twice since with no other commitments from either of them. They both had been hurt before and wanted to take it slow. I didn't interfere.

I was jolted back to the present by the waiter passing me the desserts menu.

"You don't want any." She decided for me looking at my paunch.

I shrugged and ordered one anyway.

"We will share," I said in answer to her stare.

"Why wait for him to breakup with you?" I asked next.

"I can't be the one to hurt someone again." She repeated what she had said a year back.

I sighed and took her hand from where it lay on the table.

"Maybe that someone you keep referring to deserved to be hurt," I said as my fingers found way between hers.

"No one does," she replied.

We kept looking at each other in silence, still holding hands oblivious to our surrounding till the waiter interrupted by clearing his throat, serving us a single sizzling brownie between us.

I smiled at her as I picked up the fork.

"This is you." I served her the hot brownie. "This is me." I followed it up with the vanilla ice cream. "You need me to cool you down."

She indeed had calmed down.

"That makes him the chocolate sauce," she giggled and I shrugged.

"He is good for you," I declared next.

"I know," she replied, "And we are cheesy," She laughed at my analogy.

We continued making small talk till the bill arrived and then I dropped her home, like yesterday and the day before that and the day before. Like every day.

An hour later I was back home to the other end of the city. Like always I messaged her a single word, *reached*, and she replied with *GN*.

Like always, I was online after half an hour and so was she.

Like always, I was playing Spider solitaire and waiting for an alert.

Like always I was waiting for her to finish the Skype call

with him.

He is not coming for another three months at least, she typed.

Hmm, I typed back.

That sucks, she wrote next.

I know, I typed.

Should I break up with him? she asked me.

He is good for you, I wrote.

I know. But it's so complicated.

It's not if you don't make it complicated.

She didn't reply.

You have seen complicated. Trust me this is simple; I wrote after five seconds.

Join a dance class with me, she wrote next followed with a smile emoticon.

You are not using this to blackmail me into a dance class, I wrote, she replied with a grin.

GN, Palash, she wrote.

GN.

She was offline.

And I started playing Solitaire again. To put it all back in neat stacks. Backwards…

Starting with ones and twos… and ending with the Jacks, Queens and Kings.

I would like to believe I was the King.

Chapter 3

Strike One

Not meeting you today in the evening. I found someone to join me for dance class. Going to check it today. I woke up to her SMS.

K, I typed and with that got ready for office.

She wasn't free in the evening and that meant I was.

Squash six p.m. @ the club? I sent the text to the only other person I could tolerate after her.

He sent me the thumbs up.

All people around me were so-called men of few words.

Like always, Varun picked me from office in his swanky BMW. A car I had started to envy and was the only thing I was tempted to buy in years.

"So, she ditched you today?" he said as soon as I was in the car.

"She is checking out some dance class," I stated as I put on my seat belt.

"Ahh…!" he exclaimed. "Hence you remember me. That's awfully mean of you."

I didn't reply.

"I am just a fall back when she isn't around. And then you call me a friend." He went on regardless.

"Don't start again," I said as I closed my eyes and rested my head against the car head rest signaling an end of conversation. Except, he didn't take it.

"You know, she is like a leech, slowly sucking the blood out of you." He went on, "Look at you man! You were the dude in college. And now, you have this." He enunciated with a hand on my stomach and then went on, "You have no interest in life. You don't pay attention to what you wear. The way you appear to people. That's no way to live."

The reading between his lines was 'look at me! I am so successful today' I ignored which further infuriated him as he was unable to extract a reaction from me.

"You were the college topper, Palash. What was I? I barely managed to clear my exams. But then you let up. All because of her. I am telling you she is a leech."

I was spared by my cellphone ringing. I picked up to a telemarketer, hoping that when I would be done, Varun will be out of his mood. He wasn't.

"And what is your problem with technology? People are using the latest iOS and you are stuck with this phone from Stone Age."

I rotated my old sturdy Nokia in my hand.

"It works."

"I am sure it does. But you as an engineer should understand radiations, the newer models are better. Also, aren't you concerned about your image? You own a business; you need to adhere to your brand image."

"My phone has got nothing to do with her, I just appreciate the simple things in life; lest you come back to her." I winked at him.

He shot me a dirty look. "Leech I tell you," he said as he turned his car into the club parking.

"Leeches only suck out the bad blood," I declared as we

took our rackets out from the trunk.

He just swayed his head in disappointment. Somehow, I had a knack of disappointing everyone.

I had two missed calls from her by the time I finished playing, some hours later.

"Shall we have dinner?" Varun was asking as I called her back.

"Can't," I mouthed to his headshake.

I made plans to meet her for dinner as we walked back to his car. Varun kept a distance from me, walking few steps ahead of me while I was on the phone.

"See that's what I meant," he said when I was done. "She has you wrapped around her little finger."

I didn't want to explain it to him. What's that saying about not wanting to dignify his thoughts with a response? I kept silent.

It was not that I was dropping all plans to be with her. It was because I chose to be with her. Whatever we had was simple. And any day I would choose her radiant company over Varun's boastful one. He won't get it. So, I chose to not explain. Maybe it was selfish on my part.

"Where should I drop you?" he asked as he sat on the driving seat. I replied with the restaurant location.

"Doesn't your dream girl ever cook?" he said sarcastically and then replied to his own question. "Oh yes, I forgot she was divorced for the same reason."

"Cut it out, Varun," I replied, a bit provoked and that gave him the satisfaction of getting to me.

He smirked in response.

"What? Wasn't it one of the reasons?" he asked.

"Her husband didn't deserve her," I replied composing

24

myself.

"And now you do?" he asked.

"I am not out to get her."

"Wake up, Ash." Varun used the nickname for me from back in college.

We drove in silence till the restaurant. He dropped me a few meters before the restaurant.

"At least say hi," I requested but he wasn't interested.

"I don't need to," he said and drove off but not before his parting comment. "Ash, you are thirty-eight, get a hold of your life."

I nodded. In his eyes, I had no idea where I was going with my life. In my eyes, I didn't care.

"Was it Varun?" she asked as I walked toward her waiting outside the restaurant.

I nodded.

"Still cannot face me, is it?" she asked and I didn't reply.

"I seriously wonder how you guys are still friends," she remarked.

"The way we are." I smiled at her and we walked inside. She spent the next hour telling me about the dance class. Technically she had attended the class for half an hour, but her narration started from the moment she had left office and ended when she took a rickshaw to the restaurant, embellished with all her thoughts, her footnotes and observations of all the people she met.

That was her. She was opinionated, judgmental and quick to jump to conclusions. But isn't it better than being cold, unresponsive?

I listened.

The desserts menu came and I glanced through it against

her disapproving looks.

"I played squash for more than an hour; I deserve a dessert." I explained myself and she shrugged.

"Shall we walk home?" she asked as we came out of the restaurant. I didn't tell her that I was already tired after the game but continued walking beside her.

"Aren't you in a hurry to reach home?" I asked with her Skype call on my mind.

"He is away on some conference." She read my mind.

We sat on a bench beside the road, halfway from her home.

"Varun still hates me," she said as a matter of fact.

"He does," I replied and she fake hit me.

"Some courtesy."

"What?" He really does hate you," I repeated and she hit me again.

"Gawd." She went nostalgic. "What days we had!"

I remained silent.

"You remember that time when we had smuggled you and Varun at our PG accommodation."

I nodded. "And next day, you were thrown outside the building."

She burst out laughing and I joined her too.

"You kept shouting at the owner that I wasn't your boyfriend." I joined her reverie.

"Well, you weren't. She just wouldn't listen. I hardly knew you back then. You were just Varun's nerdy friend."

"I did help you with a new flat though," I reminded her.

"Your Richie rich parents did. Technically."

We both went silent, each on our trip down memory lane.

"You really were wild," I remarked after some time.

"Yeah, that's why I am where I am today," she said and

26

looked at me.

I took her hand as a sign of assurance.

"It takes courage to be where you are," I assured her. "Not many people have the courage to live their lives on their own terms. Putting their foot down and saying enough."

"That's a nice way of saying, you are a bitch." She laughed.

"That's the problem… If you praise me for these attributes, I become the hero. If I praise you, it becomes negative."

She sighed and got up.

"I will not become a feminist on this. I would just say, that's life."

"So, you choose to be a defeatist," I remarked.

"I prefer realistic," she said and started walking again.

I kept sitting on the bench.

She looked back after sometime and gestured me to join her.

"Goodnight, girl," I yelled and motioned the other way to my house.

She waved and walked away without looking back even once.

I kept looking at her back for a while before walking back home myself with the memory of my first meeting with her playing on my mind.

A wild girl with a pixie cut and about a dozen finger rings. She was the room mate of Varun's girlfriend, Nisha. Varun and I knew each other since childhood. We went to Boarding School together.. Nisha was his coy, feminine girlfriend. I think the only reason he liked her was because as college friends she brought tasty home cooked meals which she always claimed was cooked by her. For Varun that quality held a very high weightage in a life partner. He was apprehensive when Nisha shifted with her. He was worried that she would be a bad influence on his homely girl.

The first time I had seen her was at the movies. Varun had booked late night show tickets and Nisha had tagged her along. Guess she didn't trust him enough. Varun wasn't a trustworthy character anyway. I was tagged along to provide some company to her and some privacy to the couple.

Twenty years back too, she was as confident as today. She had shaken hands with me and given me a broad smile, which for a guy from all-boys school was reason enough to take notice.

I had spent the duration of the movie and the dinner that followed listening to her. I remembered her radiant smile and her easy demeanor. And no, I wasn't in love with her. I was just impressed. She wasn't the kind of girl I wanted to marry at eighteen.

We had danced the night away at a disco. Again, I was impressed by her moves.

You used to love dancing; I messaged her as I reached home.

I did, she replied back.

What made you stop?

Life. Don't you remember? she replied back.

And then I did remember. She wanted to dance at her wedding. Rehearse a song and dance it out with her husband. It didn't work out under the pressure of the traditional outlook of the in-laws.

She stopped with no support from her husband.

Like I said, he didn't deserve her.

I was asleep as soon as I reached home.

Chapter 4

Cheating

I absolutely dread weekends. I am at loss right from the morning as to how to bring an end to this day. She is the social type. Sometimes she visits her family, some weekends she volunteers at a local old age home. I am not the kind of person to accompany her to both these places. I doubt if her family even knows about us being in touch. And as for the old age home, I wasn't quite the give back to society kinds. Usually, I spent the weekends finishing daily chores and catching up on sleep.

I woke up quite late on Sunday, after spending major part of last night playing Spider solitaire. We don't usually call each other on weekends. On rare occasions she comes down for an indoor movie and dinner. It turned out to be a rare Sunday. I wasn't doing too well due to viral when she called.

"My sister cancelled on me," she informed me, this meant she was free too.

"You free for a movie?" she asked next and I sneezed in response.

"Can't. I would rather rest," I informed her before going back to bed.

An hour later she was at my door with packets of instant soup.

"This is the best I can do," she informed me, holding up

instant noodles and soup.

"You didn't have to," I fake complained.

"Who else would come to take care of you?" she asked and I had no answer. She was right. No one would.

Hours later we were lying in the living room, binge watching her favorite TV series. I was in and out of naps.

"Palash." She called my name after a few episodes of her TV series.

"Hmm," I said with my eyes still closed.

"Is me hanging out with you cheating?"

Her mind frequently went on wild trips and on occasions like this it was my responsibility to bring it back to sanity.

"What do you think?" I asked instead.

She didn't reply. I woke up and sat straight with the blanket still around me.

"What happened?" I asked her as I knew her question had to have a background story.

She didn't reply.

"Did he say anything?" I asked next. She didn't reply.

This would be the right time to explain the dynamics between us. Aneesh worked in a company that supplied computer hardware to my company and it was through me that he met her some years back. He knew we were good friends and that was the latest information I had about his thoughts for us. I did not see any reason for her question.

Her silence told a different story though.

"He did say something," I stated.

"Not directly. But he keeps on dropping hints. I am not naive to not understand what he means," she revealed at last.

That unnecessarily provoked me.

"I think we are mature enough to take our decisions. We

aren't teenagers anymore," I said a bit harshly.

"Emotions and feelings don't change with age. We just find ways of dealing with them."

"So, what's your solution?" I asked.

Maybe this was the end of whatever we had between us. Maybe this whole exercise of me trying to put us in neat stacks was futile. It had to end here with stupid mismatched cards lying on top of each other.

"I don't know. You finding a girlfriend would help," she said with a wink.

"I am thirty-eight. Guess I am way past that stage."

"Finding love doesn't need an age. At least try."

I sat up straight and decided to set it straight once for all.

"You of all people should know how badly I suck at being a husband. This is what I am good at. Being there. Marriage brings in expectations which I end up not fulfilling. I have walked that path once, never again. I am not made for romantic relationships."

"You can try."

"And end up screwing someone's life again?" I questioned.

"You didn't screw anyone's life," she stated.

I laughed at that.

"Listen, don't push me into something I know I am not capable of handling just because your boyfriend is jealous of us and you want to keep your cake and eat it too. The door is wide open. You can leave. You are free to make your decisions. Just don't coerce yours on mine." I exploded.

Before I had a chance to retract, she got up and walked with the dirty dishes to the kitchen.

She came back with a glass of lukewarm water.

"Drink," she commanded as I took the glass from her hand.

I was still fuming.

"Also, you have snot up your face." She smiled.

I hurriedly cleaned it up as she burst out laughing.

"All this attitude and angry man talk doesn't work when your nose is swollen and red and especially when you have snot on your face."

I laughed a bit too.

She again sat beside me, took the glass from my hand and took my hand in hers.

"I will walk when I want to. You know that," she stated.

"This isn't cheating," I replied.

"I know."

"Besides everyone cheats. It is not possible to find all the qualities of a friend, a mentor and just a shoulder to cry on in one person. Marriages fail because we try to find everything in that one person."

"Don't generalize. Marriages work too," she refuted.

"Always the romantic," I remarked.

"Yes," she replied proudly. "See, you cannot take the guilt trip of screwing someone's life. Everyone dusts themselves up back in the saddle." She smiled at me.

"So, you are saying I didn't screw up anyone's life?" I needed that assurance more than a decade after a failed marriage.

"No, you didn't," she assured me.

"Then why is it that my ex-wife is sitting next to me, taking care of me, holding my hand and asking me if this is cheating?"

"That's pretty screwed up." She laughed.

I freed my hand from hers.

"What happened between us?" I asked.

"Not again Palash. We decided we won't walk that way,"

she reminded me.

"I know."

We were quiet for a long time.

"We let up, Palash," she said.

"I was not there for you," I stated.

"You were. You just never stood up for me."

I was thrown back to the second year of our marriage, with her yelling those exact same words at me.

"You never stand up for me!" She was shouting. Her eyes were swollen after hours of crying and her hair was a mess. She looked fifty at all of twenty-six. I was tired too.

It was the year I had left my job to start my own business.

I had walked out.

This time, I just nodded. "I screwed up."

"We screwed up," she replied. "But as you said, we are good at this, being there."

I smiled.

"I won't have it any other way," I remarked.

"Me neither."

She left when I was asleep. I woke up at night and checked my phone for the time. It was eleven p.m. and I had slept through the better part of the day.

There was a message from her. *More soup in the microwave. Sorry can't afford killing you with my cooking. Order something.*

I wasn't hungry. I reheated the soup and then like every day I was online. She was too.

How do you feel now? she asked.

Better, I lied.

How's Aneesh? I asked next.

He says he knows I need someone because he can't be

there. And he says once he is back, I won't have such thoughts.

So, he approves the cheating? I joked

Everyone cheats, she quoted me.

I was back to my game. This time it didn't take that long to put it back to the start of the pile of cards neatly stacked. Guess I had cracked a code of putting it back together.

Without hints. Without cheating.

Chapter 5

Limits & Continuity

Facing her after I lose my cool is always a problem. I had made a few promises to myself, not losing my cool with her was one of them. The other promises included not raising my hand, not getting too involved with anyone and alike. Now that the cat is out of the bag, it is time to accept that I was a man who did all the above things without the not. I was that person. I was that husband who didn't deserve her or anyone in fact. I was that man who did more than play squash and solitaire. I was a man who had a social life.

Maybe I am being too harsh on myself. Trust me, this isn't a guilt trip. This isn't even a trip where I redeem myself. There's no redemption. There's no forgiveness. The fact remains that I was that person.

People don't really change the way they are. They just find ways to deal with it. Somehow fit in. I did too.

And the decision happened the day we decided to sign the papers. I don't understand human psychology but I feel the emotions proceed from anger, helplessness to calmness. Nothing but calmness.

We had our roller coaster ride for the two years we managed to be married to each other. I cannot pinpoint a single episode that triggered the end. But I think we both would agree that we ducked at being married. It isn't an autocorrect.

We really ducked. We ducked responsibilities, we ducked expectations and when things started going wrong, we ducked discussions to set it right. The end result being that we sucked at being a married couple. We fucked up.

We were everything we were not as friends. This story however is not an explanation of how things went wrong between us. I am sure if she wrote it, it would be a totally different story. So, I will not go there. For my own sanity, I won't.

I would however concentrate on how and why she became my pronoun.

Like I said, the emotions range from anger, helplessness to calmness.

"I cannot take this anymore. Saying everything I said before," she said and somehow, I was so indifferent to her that I didn't concentrate on what she wanted to say, instead what I heard were Linkin Park lyrics and I mentally added the music. I ducked being a good listener.

I didn't respond.

"I want out."

This was a conversation that followed almost every fight we had.

"Okay," I responded. The usual way was that we would fight, she would give up, we won't talk for a couple of days, I would come home with a bouquet and then just like that we would be friends again. Till the next fight.

And that's perfectly normal for any normal married couple. That's how people stay married. I forgot one small detail though. Normal.

She was anything but normal. And I knew that when I got myself in. Even I was looking for something beyond normal at that point. I had been a witness to the tasteless marriage between Varun and Nisha, where a well-educated girl was reduced to an excellent chef. From what I saw, Nisha's cooking was holding their marriage together.

Ours was torn apart by the lack of it.

"Why can't you cook normal food like Nisha?" I remarked one night after we both had reached home after twelve hour shifts.

She looked hurt. That was one of the many fights. We didn't talk for few days and then like always when I brought the bouquet, she opened her heart to me.

"I wasn't hurt by the expectation. I think it is a valid point, we eat takeaways almost every day. I should cook, even though I hate it. I was hurt by the comparison."

"I just said it. I didn't mean it," I replied like always. If I have to write a book on how to survive a confrontation with a female I think I would write say 'I didn't mean it' In golden letters. It works.

"Except you did," she replied.

"Anyway, I have some points about you too. Why can't you be like Varun and buy me jewelry every month? I would love to be pampered like that," she refuted.

I snorted.

"Varun is a millionaire. I am not. And you are not a bimbette who sits at home. You earn. Save and buy it yourself. You don't need a man for that," I replied.

She patted my back with a knowing look.

"Exactly!"

I can bet women can be great lawyers. At least she was.

"Stop manipulating me," I shouted at her in my head as I calmly threw the packing of the take-away.

We had many of such fights. There was no final straw or anything. It just died a natural death where she claimed she couldn't take it anymore and walked out.

We didn't meet for about six months where the man I was told me that she would come to her senses and come back home.

She didn't.

I had moved from anger to helplessness.

We met next to sign the papers. A relationship gone sour because we ducked.

When she came home to pick her stuff, I helped her pack.

"What went wrong?" I asked her as she put the boxes in the car.

"We were great friends Palash. We should have continued being that," she replied calmly. She was there before I was.

"Wasn't friendship a basis of our marriage?"

"Yes, but we didn't build on it," she replied.

I was helpless but I was accusive. I had this inherent urge to redeem myself. To place the blame. I married the wrong girl.

"You changed," I accused. "You acted so independent and modern when we were friends. And as soon as we got married it was all about expectations." I had no idea what I was saying but went on regardless. "You were just like Nisha. What's the difference then?"

She just smiled.

"Every relation has a limit. I cannot demand from a friend what I can from a husband. I think we both forgot to make sure we were on the same page."

She tried explaining but then gave up. "Anyway, like I said, we were and will remain good friends."

She was gone as I sat in a house which looked as if it was suddenly made to strip down to its bare minimum. I felt the same. The reality sank in that day.

That was the first and last time that I cried for her. And I wasn't that man any more. I turned into what I am today.

And she is still her. There is no way to modify perfection. She always was perfection. She still fights, she still speaks her mind. She still walks off when she is done. She still takes care of me. She still is perfection.

There are no regrets though. As she said, we were great friends and we continue being that.

It comes back to me, putting our life in neat stacks from chaos. The suits remain the same. I just find ways to deal with them.

Chapter 6

Owning the Breakup

The first meet post a breakup is when you try to own the person. Somehow prove the other that you are doing well. That you have moved past them. That you survived.

We met next when Nisha thought it would be a great idea to invite both of us together for a Sunday brunch in an effort to fix us, put us together again. It was a disaster, for her. I don't know why we went ahead with it. Some people in our lives demand that kind of deference.. Nisha was like that. We always did what she expected out of us. Not out of fear but out of her genuine kindness. She was the reason we both landed for that brunch in the presence of the obnoxious Varun who now had another upper hand in form of a successful personal life, something he didn't forget to wave in front of my face. I had no idea when he started the mental competition, but it existed and every little victory mattered to him. As much as it didn't affect me.

She walked in the house in an old faded tee and battered jeans. The same clothes I had seen her wear for five years in college.

I went with my best clothes on. I had to own it.

The morning was pretty awkward with Varun and Nisha trying to fill in all the gaps. I helped by blabbering about my successful business and the progress I was making. She remained unfazed.

And then I overhead her talking to Nisha in the kitchen.

"Look at you, and look at him," Nisha said. "It looks like you are the only one suffering."

I had managed to portray the win.

She smiled.

"I am not suffering. I am just being myself again. And he is the one still trying to be someone he is not."

"I don't get you guys," Nisha interrupted her. "How does it matter? I think you guys are just being childish. Compromises are done by everyone. Why are you putting so much of emphasis on yourself?"

"I don't expect you to get me, Nisha. No one does," she replied as she noticed me overhearing and walked past me.

I followed her.

This was the first time we were meeting, the only thing I wanted was to hold her hand and tell her to come back home. I was done with the facade. But Varun's presence made me a different person. I did not say anything.

Varun kept passing snide remarks at her throughout the brunch.

"Nisha makes the best continental food," he said with his mouth full. "Bet you don't even know what the ingredients are," he directed at her.

She just smiled.

"She hates cooking, Varun," Nisha defended her. "I bet I would be that bad at all the finance stuff she manages."

"For that you have me." He gave her a flying kiss. All his antics were to portray a happy couple void of any shortcomings. "What would a man do, if his wife doesn't even know how to cook?" He laughed at his own joke.

She joined the laughter.

"I don't know, Varun. Divorce her maybe…" she joked. "Oh wait, we should ask Palash what he did with his unqualified wife."

And I exploded.

"Don't blame me, you walked out. I was happy eating Chinese and pizzas every day," I countered.

It's funny how the only reason I now remember for our separation is the least important one. It might seem that we got divorced because she couldn't cook. It wasn't even a reason. Frankly, I failed to see what the reason was. I was happy. Who doesn't fight? Everyone fights and then moves on. That's life.

For her though, there always was a bigger picture.

There always was a philosophical way to every trivial fight. Our every fight ended up with her conclusion that I wasn't doing enough for her.

"See that's the problem with city girls," Varun went on. "It's always about me, me, feminism and all that crap. That's why we are leading toward the west. No good old values," he went on.

The independent, strong-willed person that she was, listened because that person had the values of honoring the host.

The jerk that I was listened too because I was hurt and someone else was doing the job of hurting her back for me.

She glanced at me.

"I don't expect you to stand up for me now, when you never did when we were married," she told me.

"What would he say?" Varun answered for me. "You spoilt the life of a perfectly normal man, and now you expect laurels?"

Nisha wanted to interrupt for her friend; but her friend always knew how to stand up for herself. She stopped her even before Nisha opened her mouth.

"There's this funny little liberty in being the outcast here." She laughed. "I no longer have to nod and agree to all the crap happening here. I am not bound to anyone. So, I can walk out." She pecked Nisha's cheek and was collecting her bags.

"Please don't leave," Nisha pleaded.

"I really love you, girl, but not more than I love me, as your husband just pointed out," she replied.

"I told you, Palash. Don't marry the tramp. You won't listen. See she has no regrets." Varun wouldn't give up.

She smiled, looked at Nisha and repeated her earlier words.

"Nish, see how much I love you? Take care." She chose not to respond to Varun's hurtful words for her love for Nisha.

Without a second glance at me, she was out of the building.

Varun sat there complacent with his performance. Nisha stood looking at the open door. And I sat there with my head in my hands, because I never learnt to stand up for myself or her.

Nisha looked at me, waiting for my response. Something within me snapped, a bit too late but it did. All these opinions about her were held by my family too. I had never stood up for her, because I was caught between being faithful toward my first family and her. I had chosen to be with her, accepting her for what she was. It shouldn't have mattered to her what anyone else thought of her. That's what I told her always. But now as I saw a third person tear her apart, something within me tore too. I suddenly understood how she felt when my family kept hammering the same things to her. I suddenly understood a bit too late though that for her, my family was that third person with me being the only link. The only link she wished stood up for her. The only link who failed her always. I expected her to accept my family as her own, and she did. But I failed to see

43

that deep inside they still and would always be my family for her. The way Varun was her best friend's husband for her, for whom she chose to not respond to his verbal assault.

I saw it all in response to Nisha's glance at me. She kept looking at me to say the right thing.

"You had no right, Varun," I said finally. "You will never blame her or bad mouth her again, if we have to remain friends." I stood up finally.

Nisha smiled at me and hugged me.

I walked out too. Her battered clothes weren't a sign of her defeat, they were a sign of her being the girl I knew and married again. Of her being herself.

She really had moved on and finally managed to teach me something I failed to see while we were together.

She owned the breakup.

Chapter 7

Survival

I woke up to loud banging of the door, followed by the shrill of the doorbell and cries of my name in her voice.

I took some time to gather myself and land myself from outer space to my apartment.

"Where the hell are you?" she shouted as I opened the door.

"Home. What happened?"

"What happened?" she repeated in a sarcastic tone. "What happened is that you are out of contact from last forty-eight hours. Not picking calls. Not going to office… What are you up to?" she questioned looking around the room which had nothing else but the carpet on which I laid moments earlier. I could see the blinking from my phone that signaled the missed calls.

"Nothing happened," I replied again lying down on the carpet, "just taking some time off."

She stood with her hands on her hips, ready to judge me.

"Anything wrong with that?"

"Do it, but at least have the decency to inform the people who care."

I snorted.

"Where? Who?" I questioned.

She pulled my blanket at that with some swearing. "Get up Ash, I am not letting you wallow in self-pity. Get over yourself. What's wrong with you?"

I resisted all her efforts.

"Nothing is wrong. I just need some time for myself. Go away."

And she left.

When I called her the next day, she didn't take my call.

I messaged her to call me.

She ignored.

I am sorry, I texted her next, *waiting for your call*. I had a long wait as she messaged me the next day.

Your behavior doesn't make any sense to me.

I know, I replied.

Do you still love me?

Don't please yourself. No, I replied back.

Then act thirty-eight.

Don't you get your lows? I asked her next.

I do. But I sail past without bothering others.

I didn't reply.

It's my sister, I replied after a while. *She had the audacity to create a profile in my name on marriage portal.*

I finally revealed the reason.

We need to meet; I cannot react to this on text, she texted back.

Same time. Same place.

After office, I picked her up and as soon as she saw me, she burst out laughing.

"This is your reaction?" I asked sarcastically.

"What else you expect from Palak? She always looks out for you."

"I don't expect to be fixed like this," I exclaimed, and she laughed a bit.

It was a Friday and like all Fridays we rode to HRC and

were seated in the outdoor area where I could smoke freely.

"Why don't you want to be fixed?" she asked me next.

"I am done with the whole marriage thing." I spoke my mind.

"Don't make me the monster, Ash. Did I really break you this bad?" she questioned, and I gave her a sarcastic look.

"You really need to come back to earth. Aneesh might be good for you, but he is turning you into a narcissist."

"Oh, I thought I always was that," she replied with a smile and to punish her I exhaled the smoke in her direction which she waved away. She hated my smoking. I had tried to quit when we were married and anyway avoided it in her company. But Fridays were for unwinding and she didn't mind.

"It's been a decade Ash, maybe what Palak wants is good for you." She tried to convince me. I didn't respond.

"What if you really find a sweet, homely girl who wants to spend her life taking care of you through this?" she asked me next.

"I never wanted a homely girl. I married the one I wanted when I wanted and I think that's enough for a lifetime."

"Are you seriously giving me the crap of we live only once, die only once, love only once?" She imitated the actor.

"What movie was that?" she asked even before I could answer.

I didn't answer.

"Self-indulgent again," I said instead.

"Look me in the eye and tell me you don't love me," she said next, and I did exactly as told.

Like I said when I began this. I wasn't any more.

"Then go ahead with what your sister wants."

"It's always a yes, no situation for you, isn't it? If I don't want this, I have to want that."

47

"That doesn't make sense. What do you want?"

"I don't want to be pushed. I want to do things when I want to do them, when I am ready. Not because Palak thinks we need an heir or because you think I need to be fixed up," I went on blabbering.

"This just isn't happening again. I am happy with my life as it is now. So, no one messes up with it anymore," I concluded.

"And what will you do when I move to U.S.A.?" she asked me.

"Why will you move?"

She gave me the understanding look, waiting for me to catch up. I didn't because I didn't want to.

"Aneesh is not moving back to India. So, if I want us. I will have to move," she said.

"So now you are the kind of girl who moves continents for her guy?" I teased her.

She took a deep breath before replying.

"No, Ash. I am the kind of woman who knows what she wants, who is not living in a time capsule, who knows that life isn't about that one great love story. That as humans we err, we move on and we deserve to be happy. Life is about choices that you make, chances you take. And I am ready to take my chance with Aneesh. Maybe I will be sitting here with you in ten years' time and another failed marriage. But I am willing to take that risk. Question is, are you?"

I had no answer. Was I willing to let go of her. Let go of whatever arrangement we had. She was always the one. If not a wife, a confidante, my best friend. Was I ready to give her place to someone else? Was I even ready to open my heart to welcome someone in my life? Would that someone even fill the void she would leave.

"You claim to not love me, Ash. Even I claim the same. Because for us to survive, we need to keep telling ourselves this. We aren't love-struck teenagers anymore. We are adults who deserve a happy ending."

"And that's not together." I finished her thought.

"That's not together," she repeated.

"You want a walk through?" she said after a while.

She didn't wait for my answer.

"The first thing we will do if we decide to give ourselves a second chance is make a list of do's and don'ts based on what went right or wrong the first time."

"And the moment our relationship becomes a list, we are doomed," I filled in.

"We are doomed," she repeated.

We sat in silence for a while.

"When do you move to U.S.?"I asked her next.

"I don't know. Depends on the processing time, I am looking for a job there."

"What will you do after I am gone?" she asked next.

"What I did before you came in my life," I replied. "Live. SURVIVE."

She placed her hand on mine. She was everything since we turned eighteen. Twenty years of my life with her presence. With at least the knowledge that she was a phone call away. Will I survive without that knowledge? She was my pronoun and I wasn't prepared to replace her with anyone. Even when later I did find Amrita, she was her. Amrita was Amrita, she wasn't my pronoun. I had no claim on Amrita the way I had on her.

She was my pronoun.

"I don't love you," I said with my eyes full.

"Me neither," she replied.

Chapter 8

Neat Stacks

I promised this is going to simplify and it still would. All of this has to make sense, fall into stacks from the chaos. And if I am the one telling this story, I should be the hero. I should be the king. Except that I am not. I am just a mute spectator to my own life. I am the feather carried by wind irrespective of my own willingness to be blown.

Regardless, I intend on fulfilling all my promises. I may deter but I will fulfill my commitments, a thing I learnt from her, again a bit too late.

It was the time after we had already separated. The timeline was about a year after the ill-fated lunch effort by Nisha. We still had a lot of venom against each other. At least I did. I never understood her. She always acted neutral. Maybe she wasn't that affected by me or the failure of our marriage. Something that troubled me then. I had to matter to her and she behaved like I didn't.

We crossed paths professionally after deliberately avoiding each other for more than a year. She had texted me asking for help on hardware information that her company needed. She was a finance person. I texted her back Aneesh's number a day too late to seem busy.

The next time we met was in a party thrown by Aneesh to celebrate the order he received from her company through me. I don't know what made me go. Maybe it was yet another effort to win the breakup. In retrospect, I was jealous of the way Aneesh kept praising her and I wanted to see if there was more to it. In fact, I was sure there was more to it, and I wanted to shame her about it. If I wasn't ready to move on, she shouldn't either.

It was a pool side party, and in my curiosity, I reached a bit too early . Only Aneesh and a few of his colleagues were around. I was the first guest. She walked in an hour later. By that time I was already wasted on the free alcohol. I was met with a stern nod from her that made me feel like being caught in a mischief by a high school principal.

Aneesh played the perfect host. We only knew each other professionally, so he wasn't quite aware of our situation until then.

"Trust me, if it wasn't for her, I would not be able to get such a good deal." Aneesh continued his praise.

I snorted and she noticed.

"I was just doing my job," she replied modestly.

"I know," Aneesh faltered, "but a great job. Usually, it's difficult to deal with the finance people. But it was a pleasure working with you." He flashed his perfect teeth at her and I knew that very instant where it was going.

I was the one doing that few years back, so I knew the routine. I recognized the smiles, the attention and the chivalry. I had done all that to win her over a few years back. Aneesh was following the routine.

"So, this is how you do it now," I said sarcastically when Aneesh left to attend to other guests.

"Don't do this, Palash. You don't need to fall so low," she warned me and in my drunken state I didn't care.

"Did I ever tell you, how I know her?" I announced when Aneesh returned.

He nodded a no.

"I was married to her," I declared a bit too loudly.

Aneesh seemed surprised but he covered it up. She winced.

"But don't worry. We are divorced now. She is back in the game," I announced again.

Her eyes pleaded with me again but I ignored.

"You know what's wonderful though?" Aneesh asked and then continued making me feel ashamed of myself. "That you guys remain good friends and even help each other out professionally. It's difficult to find such maturity."

I had no words. He was a bigger guy than what I was then.

We continued making small talk and then after I had another drink or two, she approached me as I sat sulking in a corner.

"Get up, we are going home," she ordered.

"We aren't married any more. So, I don't take orders from you," I replied back.

She sighed.

"We can do it your way and create a scene here or just sort it out in a private space. The decision is yours. But trust me, this isn't you and I am not letting you turn into this loathsome person."

I didn't reply.

"I am waiting in the car outside. Meet me in five."

And she left.

I followed her like a lost puppy.

We didn't talk the whole way home.

Only when she stopped in the parking lot of my apartment, we talked.

"Please come up," I pleaded and she nodded a no.

"This is your home too," I said again.

"Was my home, Palash," she corrected me.

That infuriated me. In my drunken state, I had no control over my emotions as they swayed between helplessness and deep-rooted hatred toward her.

"Which you left. For your ill-placed ego," I refuted back.

"As I said Palash, we can do it your way. If two years of marriage were not enough for us to fight, we can continue doing so now too."

I didn't reply.

"Or we can be the way we were before we decided to get married. We were the best of the friends Palash and I think we still can remain good friends. I will never stop caring for you," she concluded.

And I was more messed up than before. This didn't make sense.

"What went wrong?" I asked again but she didn't reply.

"Go up and go to sleep. We will talk later," she said instead and I left.

That was the day I stopped being resentful toward her and started accepting that we still could mean something to each other.

The next day, I sent her a bouquet of white roses with an apology. She replied with a text. The very same day we met for dinner.

"You look stunning," I said and she laughed out loud.

"Seriously, Palash." She laughed.

I really didn't know what to say to her any more. When we were married, it was all about balancing what she was and what my family expected out of her. When we separated, I went into

53

autopilot mode finishing all formalities without feeling a thing. For me, her deciding to leave me was the biggest blow, nothing could ever hurt me more. Or so I thought. The two times that I met her post our separation were spent in an effort to hurt her as much as she hurt me. And now when she motivated me to move forward, I didn't know what to say to her. It wasn't a fresh start. It was a journey beyond the semicolon. The complex sentence had to mean something after the semicolon, otherwise it was just the end. It just deserved a full stop. The fact that we were investing in each other and sat facing each other at dinner meant that there still was some meaning left between us. I just had to find out what.

"How do you do it, Meera?" I asked.

"Honestly. I don't know."

I didn't prod further. Just kept looking at her. She went on.

"I really want to fight with you Palash. Blame you for everything. Blame you for spoiling my life. For twisting and turning me into someone I don't recognize any more. I want to shout at you." She laughed a bit. "Trust me, there's so much of frustration inside me that I can only direct at you."

"Why don't you?" I had to ask.

"What's the use, Palash?" she replied as calmly as possible. "We spent two years of our married life doing that. It always goes in circles. We fight because we expect. I expected you to like me the way I was. You expected me to fall in line with what you wanted. We failed to find us. And that's fine. I don't want to get melodramatic about it. We sucked at marriage. But that doesn't make you or me a bad person. And I think I would be happier focusing on the good in us."

I laughed at that.

"I don't know, Meera. I have stopped believing that good

54

exists in me."

She extended her hand to place on mine.

I assumed to make me feel better.

"If that's what you really believe, maybe it's true." She winked at me.

I smiled.

"Honestly, I always thought I was the villain of our marriage," she said

"You were." This time I winked at her.

"I know Palash. And I don't know how to apologize about it." She took me seriously. "When we fought, I always tried to find where I went wrong. What I could have not said to aggravate the situation. When you hit me that one time, I tried to believe that maybe I pushed you that far. But nothing justified it, Palash. That was the only reason I moved. You asked me last night, what went wrong? This is what went wrong. I gave you a right over me to make you think anything goes. This is what went wrong, Palash. I was the villain because I failed to establish boundaries."

"I will never forgive myself for it," I confessed.

We didn't talk for a while. We finished eating and then asked for the bill.

"What now?" I asked again.

This is when she became my pronoun.

She laughed before answering. "This wasn't a counselling session Palash which we walk out of as a happy couple. When we got married, we promised each other certain things, all that in sickness and in health things. But those promises don't mean that we have to live together and make each other miserable. I made certain commitments to you with the vows and I intend on fulfilling them. Because in spite of seeing the rock bottom of each other, I personally don't hate you, nor do I think I ever could. So yes, we can choose to walk out of here deciding to not hate each other anymore. And be always there for each other. To fulfill our vows. What say?"

That's how we landed up where we are today.

Like I said, neat stacks.

Chapter 9

Second Chances

Ever wonder how irritating a door bell can get? Especially when you are drunk from last night and lay half-naked on the floor with empty beer bottles and pizza boxes around you. I peeked through the key hole and a person I wanted to meet least was standing on the other side of the door.

That too the very next day of a mental exaltation . The very next day you finally feel whole. The very next day you get the person you pine for so badly back in your life. At least I could open the door without having to clean up.

Aneesh walked in with his immaculate clothes and in one sweep registered the mess that was my house.

"I called you; you didn't pick up. I hope it is fine that I drop in," he said

It wasn't fine.

"It is," I lied and excused myself to clean up. When I returned dressed up decently, he had cleaned the room. The empty bottles were in the bin. The blanket was folded up and now the room was as immaculate as him.

I knew he meant business.

I looked around.

"I hate mess. I hope it's fine," he explained.

This time it was fine.

"Coffee?" I offered as a means to break the ice but he

refused. I waited.

He fiddled around a bit before approaching the topic of discussion.

"Listen, it's about the night before," he started off.

"I am sorry," I blurted out.

"You need not be," he cut me short. "I totally understand you."

"The place and time were wrong and I apologize."

He just nodded. I had to find a way to redeem myself. Just his presence in the room made me feel inferior.

"The thing is…" he faltered a bit more and I knew where it was going. "I know you for long professionally and I don't know if my personal decisions will affect us in future."

"It will not." I cut him short and then put into words his thoughts. "Meera and I will always be good friends. There is nothing beyond. I would always be concerned for her but what she chooses to do here on is none of my business."

I was proud of my growth as a person in one night. A pride I totally tried to bask in to cloak the deep pang in my heart.

He left.

Congratulations. You have someone who loves you more than me, I texted her soon after.

She replied with a *?*

We didn't talk for the rest of the day and many days after.

Was 'I am a bigger person' a one-off thing? she messaged a fortnight later.

What do you mean? I texted back

We never met after that one time, she replied. *I need to talk to you.*

Pick you up at nine, I replied back.

"I am freaking out, Ash," she said as soon as she sat behind me on the bike.

"Now you get it. The reason I congratulated you," I replied. I was trying to act as normal as her.

"You knew?" She was surprised.

"Aneesh met me and told me," I informed her.

"For what? Permission?" she snorted. "What am I? Some commodity?"

"Don't be so touchy. He is good guy."

She was surprised and raised her brow.

"Better than me anyway," I added

"What did you guys talk about? Terms and conditions?" She still was sarcastic.

"Sorta," I decided to provoke her.

She hit me playfully on the shoulder, understanding the pun.

"I am freaking out. I am not ready," she said after a while.

"Tell him that," I replied totally understanding her not ready comment. I wasn't ready either, I didn't know when I would be or if ever I would be.

"He said he will wait," she told me, and I hated the whole pack of good guys. We had a name for such guys back in college and in my mind I used all the sobriquets for Aneesh. I may curse him but the truth was that he was better than me. Sooner I accepted that, sooner could I get peace.

"What do you want to do today?" I asked her.

"I don't know. Escape," she replied.

We went for a late-night movie thereafter.

"Bollywood is so unimaginative," she commented as we walked home, referring to the movie.

"I already told you it would be a crap movie. You wanted to escape. So, we went."

She let that comment pass.

"But her last movie was so good. I expected it to be better," she complained again.

"The problem with Bollywood is they don't know how to handle the topic of ex-lovers," I chipped in.

"So what? Give cancer to the girl and let her die? How uncreative!"

"What else would it be? She already broke up with him. They needed a reason for her to act bitchy. A lead heroine cannot be bitchy." We continued discussing the plot of the movie. "So that's a good reason, she wants him to hate her."

"Yeah, so a fake marriage works? Be upfront. Tell the guy. This isn't working."

I fake coughed.

"What?" she exclaimed.

"Not everyone is you Meera and not everyone is me."

"What does that mean?" she asked.

"It means we are bigger actors than the movie actors. We both can keep acting like we don't love each other anymore, hoping it to turn real. They can't do that. They need closure. Cancer is a closure. Death is a closure. What we have isn't closure. What we have is lifetime torture and no one buys tickets to watch lifetime torture. We need closure."

She sighed.

"We need closure," she repeated after me. "Is not meeting each other again ever and hating each other till we die closure?" she asked next

"It's not," I panicked.

"You don't seem to be a fan of my option of being friends."

"It's lifetime torture," I repeated.

"I don't see how. We hated each other as a married couple, we rocked as friends so we go back to being friends. It's as simple as that," she repeated.

"It's not simple, Meera. What if Aneesh asks you to not be friends with me in future?"

"Is that what your real problem is Palash? We aren't teenagers any more. The very expectation of finding a brand new person at this age is stupid and I think he knows that."

"You are not getting me," I argued.

"The reason that movie had an ending was because that is an end. Where's the end for us?"

"So, you mean, you would have me rather dead?" She winked at me.

"Or vice versa."

She hit me with her clutch at that.

"I will not listen to this nonsense Palash. Like I said we aren't lovestruck teenagers. We are mature adults with a lot of water under the bridge. We hold our head high and we sail ahead."

"It's that simple for you, isn't it?" I was a bit angry now.

"Believe me nothing of this is simple. Like every normal girl even I dreamt of a happily ever after, with you. But if that wasn't meant to be. I would rather move ahead than crib or play blame games."

"You make me sound like a monster."

"No Palash. I attempt to make us realize the ground reality. There is no second chance for us. There's only one way forward and that's not together."

The reinforcement of her thoughts about our relationship continued. I suddenly was a meek follower of a path she paved for us. A path well above the rest and a path that made me a better person.

Sometimes love doesn't make you a better person. Solitude

61

does. It is only in solitude that you realize the true worth of every one in your life. She was worthy of more. She was worthy of better than me.

I was worthy of my solitude, to think, to rationalize and to find a closure.

She already had closure with her decision of moving ahead from her crappy husband. I had to find closure in not getting hung up on my not so bad wife. It's only when I lost her that I realized what I had lost. It was only when she lost me did she realize what she really wanted in life. We were both each other's experiments gone sour. The trials no one documents. The people who aren't in your life story when you reminisce over the past. Except that my story started with her and will end with her. My pronoun.

Wasn't this the very intention of starting this? Reaching the fountainhead of us, where all the droplets of our lives merge into one.

Where I become whole again.

Keep up with me, I beg. Together we reach the source.

Chapter 10

Green-Eyed Monster

"Grow up, Palash," she kind of yelled into the phone and I moved it away from my ear.

"Don't make me come down there and smack you," she continued.

I didn't reply. I was fuming. Silence was my friend. I was hoping my silence would convey everything I felt — my anger, my disappointment and my fear of losing her forever.

"You knew this was to happen. I am thirty-six," she went on.

"I won't come," I said finally.

"You would," she decided for me. "And before that we will meet today evening for dinner."

"No." I acted up again.

"Nine p.m. HRC," and she disconnected.

I threw the phone in frustration. Then for good measure threw the pillows from the bed. None of which made me feel better, so the next thing I did was put on my shoes and run till all my built-up anger was gone. Till the tears that refused to come took the form of sweat. I ran till I couldn't breathe and then increased my pace till my heart felt like it would leap out of my chest.

My mind wandered to the last time I had run this fast, years back to get her. In a clichéd love story that was ours. She was leaving the city and heading home. Forever. And in a blink I had realized I couldn't let her go. We had known each other as extended friends of Nisha and Varun. We were the plus two every time they couldn't hang out alone. Like I said before, she wasn't my type. My type was a homely girl, I had imagined since adolescence. Someone like my mom — soft spoken, clad in a saree, one who would always put others need before hers. Shy, demure. She was none of this. Nisha was all of this. But when I met them together, she always seemed to stand out. Nisha was boring. It confused me. Wasn't I supposed to be attracted toward Nisha and not her? Wasn't this what I wanted? I had to sort my thoughts out. Nisha requested Varun to drop her at the airport and he requested me to join. Till that moment I had no clue that her departure would mean something to me. Over the years we had formed a basic friendship as we had to stand each other for our friends' sake. And it worked. I used to get irritated by her outspoken nature many a time, but I didn't ever say anything to her because it wasn't my place to say anything. She wasn't anyone to me. Like that one time at dinner, she fought with the manager as he sold some cold drink above the MRP. I was embarrassed. I wasn't brought up like that.

"You could have let it go," Varun commented, obviously embarrassed too.

"Oh, I am sorry." She fake apologized. "Did I embarrass you rich kids?" she asked and got up to leave.

Varun signaled me to join her, and I followed her out of the restaurant . I had no intention of convincing her to come back. Like I said she was no one to me.

"Go back, Ash. I am sorry to embarrass you guys. But I can't stand this cheating," she said as I reached her.

"It's okay. I will walk you home," I decided. This seemed

like a better option than returning to the love birds.

We kept walking in silence.

"It was a matter of two bucks," I said after some time.

"I am a student," she replied. "I earn my own money to pay for my expenses. Two bucks matter to me."

I didn't understand her logic and so I shrugged.

"Let me guess..." she replied, "your father is a rich businessman and obviously you never earned a penny for yourself."

"Let me guess." I decided to tease her. "Your father is a bank clerk, Mom has tuberculosis. You live under leaking roofs in utter poverty."

She laughed. "No, Dad owns a garment business. Like many refugees after partition. The conditions you described were true for grandparents. So, Dad inculcated self-reliance quite early in us. I took tuitions to pay for my pocket money. He just pays our fees and buys us clothes. Bare minimum. I have been earning since I was fifteen."

I slow clapped for her.

"Who paid for this?" I took her hand and pointed at her several gold finger rings.

"My savings. Gold is investment. Plus, it fulfils my wish of wearing jewelry."

I slow clapped again and looked at her appreciatively.

"What?" she asked.

"You are wife material. You will make someone a nice, mature partner someday."

She burst out laughing.

"There is a real world out there, outside the rich brat circle where many girls like me live. I am one of many," she commented.

"If that's how you decide to accept my compliment," I said and she smiled again.

And I realized she had a very beautiful smile. This was the first time I was noticing her physical features. Her left canine was crooked and that gave her a cute smile. With that I also remembered her brash behavior which didn't match her cute looks.

"And what's the backstory behind your aggressiveness?" I asked and she reacted by looking at me with her jaw dropped.

"You think I am aggressive?" she asked and I shrugged.

"Let me count the number of fights I have witnessed since I've known you…" I started the count on my fingers

"You fought with your landlord when he asked you to vacate the house."

"What do you expect?" she exclaimed. "He wasn't giving us any notice period!"

"Technically he did," I teased her again.

"Twelve hours is not a notice period!" she shrieked.

"What do you expect from him? You broke the rules and brought 'boys' home." I air quoted for effect.

"Not boys. Men. And that's what made me angry. I was nowhere in picture. Your car broke down, Nisha invited Varun and you, why should I vacate the house."

"You didn't tell him that though. You let him assume that we both are dating you both," I reminded her.

"I value Nisha more over that balding idiot."

Another point that made her not my type. She wasn't quite respectful toward elders unless she really respected them. My girl won't use such language ever.

"And anyway, what pisses me is that he assumed. Why do people assume the worst when such things happen? And even if it did happen what was his bloody problem?"

I didn't retort to that. I was a hypocrite then.

"Anyway, aren't you now happy in your new home?"

"Thanks to you," she replied.

Nisha and she had shifted to my vacant flat in the city.

We reached the said flat then and sat in the parking lot waiting for Varun and Nisha to join us.

"So, you don't have a boyfriend?" I asked just to carry forward the conversation.

"Naah," she replied. "Relationships are overrated."

"Or is it sour grapes?" I teased her. I really was a male chauvinist pig then.

She laughed.

"Call it anything you wish."

I liked her attitude of not giving a shit about what anyone thought about her.

"You know, if you were a guy, we would be best buddies," I said.

"And that's because you don't befriend girls?" she asked and stumped me over.

"I didn't mean that," I faltered. "We could hang out more if you were a guy, I meant."

"Because if you hang out with me now, people will think we are dating?" she reacted.

I put my hands up in air in annoyance. "You are misunderstanding me. Like Varun and I, we hang out playing squash, cricket, sci-fi movies... stuff like that."

"I get it," she replied. "And I am a girl so I must not be knowing what squash is unless it's in the fridge and yeah sci-fi like what *Transformers* or *Star Wars*, or do you call *Love Story 2050* sci-fi?"

I didn't reply. She smiled.

Varun and Nisha reached by then in Varun's beat-up car, and I didn't have to reply.

We said our byes as I opened the co-driver's door and sat beside Varun.

She tapped my window and I rolled it down.

"May the force be with you, buddy. Good night," she commented with a wink.

And she walked away.

Next day I messaged her with *Squash five p.m.?*

She replied with, *I don't have the equip.*

I replied with, *Can you really play?*

No. I will get the bottle of mango squash lying in our fridge.

Your sense of humor is pathetic, I replied back.

Not as pathetic as you, she replied.

Coming or not? I replied and she sent a yes.

If it's not a date, she wrote after some time.

It sure isn't.

She was at the club at five.

"I am not too good at this. But I am not bad either," she warned me.

I handed her Varun's racket but she refused and asked for mine.

"You really do hate him, don't you?" I asked.

She just shrugged

"I am surprised you haven't pulled Nisha away from him."

"Why would I?" She shrugged again. "That's her personal life. I don't interfere in other's lives. Maybe he is good for her."

We reached the court and she really wasn't bad. We had a good two-sided match that I enjoyed.

"When did a bank clerk's daughter learn?" I decided to

68

tease her again.

In reply she took a membership card of a top-rated club from her wallet and kept it on the table. I picked it up impressed.

"We may not be loaded like your family, but we manage."

"How loaded do you really think I am?" I asked curious.

"Enough to spoil you into branded clothes and make your sister go on international vacations with friends twice a year."

"My sister?" I asked confused.

"Palak. She is my friend's friend on FB, her updates keep cropping up. She makes sure everyone knows."

"Or were you stalking me?" I teased her again.

"If that caresses your ego. By all means." She shrugged.

"So, what next?" I asked as we had our refreshments in the club canteen.

"Well, this isn't a date, so we go our separate ways now," she replied.

I looked at the watch. It was around eight.

"Dinner?" I suggested and she agreed.

"There's this sports bar..." I tried suggesting but she interrupted me.

"Just because I said yes to playing squash doesn't mean I am in a mood to sit amongst smelly men to eat. And friendship is two-ways. You have to see my side of the world too."

I agreed and she took me to a karaoke bar where she clapped for each and every performance even if it sucked badly.

"So can you sing?" she asked me and I said no.

"Frankly I am not even enjoying much," I added and she snorted.

"See this is the sexist attitude you carry." And then she mimicked me: "If you were a guy we could be good friends! So, if a girl has to not be your girlfriend but still hang out with you,

69

she needs a high level of testosterone but you fear that you will grow breasts if you enjoy one so called feminine activity!"

She exploded and I didn't know where to look. Like I said, not my kind of girl.

Regardless a year later, just an hour after Varun, Nisha and I dropped her to the airport, my heartbeat increased and I realized that I could not lose her. I was in love with her. So, like a clichéd Bollywood climax I ran back to the parking of my flat and then to the taxi stand.

I dialed her number.

"You cannot leave," I said as soon as she picked up.

"What?" She was confused.

"I am coming to pick you up from the airport. Please don't board the plane. We need to talk," I said

"Are you crazy?" she shouted on the phone. "I bought the ticket. I am getting on the plane."

"I will pay you back," I said hurriedly. "Please don't get on the plane."

"Listen, Ash, I am in the boarding line and really don't have time for whatever attack you are having. I will call you once I land," she said and before I could respond she disconnected.

I love you. Dammit. Don't board the plane, I messaged her.

When I called her again, her phone was switched off.

I went to the airport nevertheless and boarded the next plane to her home town.

I am on the plane next after yours. At least this time don't leave the airport! I texted her before boarding my flight.

As soon as I landed, I got a call from her.

"Are you fucking crazy?" she yelled at me and people around me looked at me as her voice broke out of the phone. I was still in the plane trapped between people struggling to get their hand baggage.

"Looks like I am," I said calmly. "Where are you?" I asked next.

"Baggage claim."

When I reached her, she was standing with her hands folded like a stern headmaster and I noticed her. She was wearing a T-back with a trouser which was somewhere between a harem pant and a dhoti. Her almond eyes were currently staring at me without blinking and her very straight hair was tied up in a high bun.

It was the day she stopped being Meera and became my pronoun.

I grinned. "I hate the way you dress. What is it called anyway? And I hate it when you swear. I hate it when you say something to put me down and I hate the way you feel you are in some way superior to all of us."

She was confused.

"And you took an unnecessary flight to tell me this?"

I nodded a yes and she laughed.

"Go back home, Ash. You are confused."

And then I was angry.

"See you are doing it again. Putting me down. This won't work. You need to give me some credit."

"And who says it has to work?" she said walking away from me pushing her luggage cart.

I started walking with her.

"Can you just act normal? I just said I love you."

"The question is why, Palash! Because you also just said you hate me for many things."

"I was just being honest," I replied.

71

"And you love me because…" She left the sentence open for me to complete.

"Because I do," I said and stood in front of her luggage cart. She kept looking at me.

"You love me because, I am the only option who can stand up in front of your overbearing sister and by extension the family."

"What!" I exclaimed. Palak had met her just few months back. She was in town and when she went to see their flat, she tried to throw her weight around as we owned the flat. That didn't go well with her. She wasn't the one to be put down. She had calmly taken the rent agreement out and asked Palak if she understood the legal jargons and then proceeded to read the agreement out that said that the property was rented to them and so it was wrong of Palak to act like she was doing some charity. In fact, Nisha and she were doing charity by letting her stay with them. That was the first time I had seen my sister without an answer and out of the door.

She just shrugged.

"Meera, sometimes there is no reason for things to happen. I love you and I want to spend the rest of my life with you. Yes or no?" In my mind I was doing some charity by choosing her.

She said no. And then I had spent next whole week turning that no to yes.

Presently, I stopped running when I could no longer feel my legs. I had reached the sea and I collapsed on the sand. I wasn't twenty anymore and could feel the age as I panted and tried to regain my breath.

My thoughts raced back with me from that day at the airport to her message at night that said she was getting married to Aneesh in a few weeks and then moving to U.S.

When I met her in evening, she looked radiant.

"Congratulations, madam," I said with as much of conviction I could put in.

She shook my hand and smiled.

"So, do I need to come down to sign?" I asked as I perched on the high bar stool beside her.

"Sign?" she asked confused.

"I assumed it's a court marriage," I said.

"Because it's my second?" she asked in her condescending tone that I hated.

I didn't reply.

"It's Aneesh's first and so unfair to him. We are having a traditional one."

"Great. So, you get a second chance of righting all the wrongs I did to you at our first. Living your dreams," I said sarcastically.

Technically our fights had started before marriage during the wedding preps itself. My mother had forced some traditions on her which she had to follow and she did follow them but not without resentment. She kept expecting support from me, but I didn't support her the way she wanted me to.

It was just a stupid wedding and what difference did it make if you wore a saree instead of a designer *lehenga* if the end result was to get us together.

It mattered to her. That was the time she started saying I never stood up for her. In my mind it was trivial, it wasn't for her.

"It was my day, Palash, not your mom's not your sisters but mine and you ruined it for me. Because you never thought I was entitled to this. You just crashed all my daydreams of this

73

day just to please your family."

She told me and I lost it.

"Stop trying to put me and my family down. And you had agreed to it that time? Why are you complaining now?" I had yelled back. "What should matter is that we are together, but you don't want to see it. You just want to show how many sacrifices you made ," I kept shouting and she phased out.

Her expressions were calm again. I realized in that instant that she was out of this. She had mentally checked out of our marriage.

"I can't do this, Palash. I cannot keep suffering to feed your guilt of marrying against your parents' wishes."

Before I could retaliate or shout again, she was gone.

I looked for her only when she didn't return home at night. Then I went to pick her up from Nisha's place and convinced her that things would change. I would change. She just had to return home and she did. That one time. Nothing changed. We continued fighting and we continued growing apart.

Presently, she just stared at me, waiting for me to take what I said back. I didn't.

"True. Not everyone gets second chances," she replied.

I snorted.

"You know, Palash, I try to be the bigger person, trying not to play blame games but you leave me no choice. I said this many times when we were married, and I am forced to say this now… It mattered to me that my day was my way and it mattered to me that the person I was marrying realized this. I would have blindly followed everything you asked me to then if it was what you wanted, but it wasn't what you wanted. As for you all that was immaterial so then you chose to follow what your parents wanted over what I wanted and that made me feel insignificant."

I shrugged. All that didn't matter anymore.

"Congratulations, Meera. You finally found a puppet," I said angrily and left.

I reached home still not sure of the right emotion I felt. She didn't call me again.

I knew I would have to call her and apologize but I wasn't ready yet.

What I was ready for was Solitaire. If I couldn't sort my life out at least I could sort the cards.

Chapter 11

Karma is a...

Easy — have you ever experienced easy? And not easy in a negative way, easy in a way that is synonymous with simple. What I had with her was anything but easy. It had always been that way right from the time we were awkward third wheels as Varun and Nisha dated, to the time I landed in her hometown to propose to her. I was always awkward around her, scared of losing her, scared of being made fun of. When I married her, I assumed that would change. Somehow my fear would be replaced with peace. It wasn't. Instead, it was replaced with anxiety around her, of what she might say at the most inappropriate places in front of all the people who mattered, or as I see now, I thought then mattered. I assumed I might be able to discipline her into being submissive, being respectful, and being politically correct. I ended up being a psychotic mess who swayed between the anxiety of her behavior and the fear of losing her. Does anyone deserve this mess? Isn't love supposed to bring you peace? I shouldn't be the one asking the rhetoric questions, especially when I made the mess myself. What was I supposed to do better to make her stay in love with me? To make me feel loved. We ended up being neither. She felt unloved and I felt uncared when both had the right feelings intact for each other, only we let our accusations overshadow the positive feelings for each other. And that sure isn't easy.

Amrita wasn't like that. Being with Amrita was easy. Before getting ahead of myself I should first get to the point where I was open enough to accept a new person in my life. Or as I learnt from Amrita, she was open enough to accept me, whatever the difference is, which I am told is huge.

One of many fights Meera and I had was where I called her selfish and she went on to prove how I hid behind a mask of selflessness; but in reality, was an epitome of narcissism. Not that I agreed. That particular fight escalated to her slamming the door in my face and one of the many nights I spent on the sofa. We never got over our theatrics. With Amrita there weren't any theatrics. They say one shouldn't compare two people, but how else was I supposed to know that Amrita was better for me than Meera even when I was hopelessly in love with Meera?

I had gotten over myself and walked to her apartment to apologize.

"You don't really mean the apology, Palash," she complained.

I did not.

I looked around. Her house was a mess of unopened parcels lying everywhere. The wedding preparations were in full flow.

"Where are your parents?" I asked instead, peeping inside one of the parcels. It was some suiting material.

"Gone out for shopping, you want to meet them?" she teased.

"Yeah sure, maybe I will convince them again to let me marry you like last time. I am sure they will agree." I winked back.

"They won't," she teased back. "They know their daughter needs a puppet." She took her jab at me indicating she hadn't quite forgiven me.

"That's quite true. Aneesh is the right choice for you, you say sit, he sits." I enacted the whole training the dog sequence. I wasn't giving up either.

She winced.

"Why are you here Palash? To make sure I shouldn't feel happy ever?"

I didn't reply. Why was I at her place, when I knew she would be married in a few days? What more did I expect from her?

"Am I not supposed to react too?" I asked instead.

"Please react Palash, I am waiting," she said exasperatedly. "But just take it out of your system and then at least try to be happy for me."

I was happy for her. She indeed looked better and I wasn't stupid enough to not notice it. In the later part of our marriage, she always looked exhausted. She had stopped paying attention to herself. But now the woman that stood in front of me was the one I had met many years back. She looked younger, her smile reached her eyes and her skin looked radiant against the duller version of her when she was with me. I had blamed her for her own unhappiness then. It wasn't on me, it was on her sky high, unrealistic expectations of me that made her sad. It wasn't my fault. I was always there for her. She just didn't see it. And I always said that to her, giving her *gyaan* on how every time whatever I did was somehow minuscule for her as she kept on expecting more from me. I told her after every fight, as we made up that she needed to control her anger, find peace within herself, that her behavior was unacceptable, that somehow, I was the victim not her. That I tried to be there for her but she made it difficult with her antics.

Now Aneesh was there for her. He made her happy and I

needed to make peace with that.

"I am trying," I murmured after a while and plopped on the sofa.

"I know. Please try harder," she replied and plopped next to me to lean against the sofa back and close her eyes.

"I am tired," she said with eyes still closed. I took the opportunity to observe her and say things I really meant above my ego and without any facades.

"I am really happy for you, Meera. I wish you all the happiness in the world. You deserve every bit of it." She didn't open her eyes which gave me the courage to go on. "Please bear with me as I deal with this. I thought I have you forever and that made me take you for granted, I didn't understand when I lost you. And then in past few years, I had you again and I never thought these days will be short lived, that I would have to let go of you someday."

She still didn't open her eyes but found my hand on the sofa and intertwined her fingers with mine. "You did not and will not ever lose me. I am physically moving away but we will be in touch."

"But you are moving away, Meera. No more meeting every day for dinners."

She laughed. "You never call me by my name."

I sighed. "I don't. At least don't shift continents," I said instead.

"Even if I stay, you think we will continue meeting every day, like now," she questioned instead.

I knew we wouldn't but somehow my mind did not want to deal with the information.

"Anyway, tell me how you want me to help?" I jumped up from the sofa. I needed some motive, some movement to keep myself sane. If I had to do it, I had to do it with pride.

She got up with me and handed me a visiting card.

"This is the caterer; you are in charge of the menu. Meet the person and choose."

I nodded, put the card in my pocket without a look and followed her outside the room.

"And Palash, you really don't need to do this, if you don't want to."

"Trust me, I want to. I want to give you the dream wedding you wanted." Her eyes watered up at that and she hugged me even as I hugged her tighter, refusing to let go. She did let go.

"Not everything that's broken can be mended," she said philosophically and went inside again.

I walked out of her apartment with her thoughts behind me, trying hard to push her in my past and a card in my pocket which became my future. Amrita.

I called the caterer after a few hours of meeting her and a low base voice was at the other hand, like the person I was talking to had cold.

"I am in charge of handling the menu for the wedding. When can I meet you?" I introduced.

She cleared her throat before replying, "Yes, Meera ma'am told me you will call. Aneesh sir and Meera ma'am have already tasted our sample food, but for you we can hold another tasting session," she went on without a pause.

Just hearing their name together made me feel jealous again and the fact that they were choosing things together for their day. I was thrown back to the preparatory phase of my marriage.

"When are we choosing the menu for the guests?" Meera had asked me.

"Oh, didn't I tell you?" I replied nonchalantly. "Dad's

friend is in catering business; he already finalized the menu."

Now I could understand that she was disappointed, but then I had assured her, told her to relax.

"So, what is being served?" she had asked next.

"Who cares?" I had replied. "Why don't you just relax, there are people to take care of everything. You as a bride should not worry. Take your rejuvenation spa or whatever there is as a bridal package and relax." I was taking care of her. My family had all the connections and in my opinion, she shouldn't have sweated the small stuff.

She was used to fighting her own battles, taking all her decisions on her own, I was always taken care of and seriously, who cared what the guests ate? It was only after marriage that she shared an anecdote to illustrate her perception, to show her disappointment as being the outsider in her own marriage.

It was again the next morning of our infamous fight. I was sleeping on the sofa after the shouting at each other session of the previous night and she had called me back to the bedroom many times but I refused to highlight my anger. At dawn, she had come to cuddle, even I had gotten over my anger after sleeping over it.

"I was a guest at my own wedding, Palash," she complained cuddling against my shoulder.

"You cannot keep living in the past. Maybe I made some bad choices then, but I managed things as I could. We should look ahead, if we go on repeating the same things of what went wrong, we are ruining our present and our future." I had given her *gyaan* from my side.

"It's not things, Palash. And we are not fighting over what happened in past. We are fighting over how differently we both view things. Those incidents are just examples of the basic

81

difference in our upbringing."

"Obviously, two people cannot be same. We are different. Why are we even discussing this?" I was starting to lose my cool again. It was her condescending tone that I hated, it made me feel small. It made me feel as if she thought I was an idiot.

"You know, as kids Dad always took us Diwali shopping and we had to buy new clothes, shoes etcetera," she went on with her anecdote which was supposed to end with a moral. I already switched on my 'here it goes again' mode with a roll of my eye. Now as I look back, I understand that I spent little effort in understanding her but all effort in molding her to my needs. And this is a lesson every science person knows, to mold someone you need to first understand the inherent properties of any matter. You cannot expect ice by boiling water, ice needs cooling, ice needs patience. Throughout my marriage, I expected her to be the ice cube while heating her up with provocations from my family and me. It was never going to work.

She went on with her story, ignoring my eye rolling.

"So, I was always headstrong, I chose my own shoes. I liked the ones with studs and high heels and Mom said don't buy them, you cannot walk on high heels. Your feet will hurt, the shoes aren't comfortable, but I didn't give in. So, Dad stepped in and bought those shoes for me and damn they hurt as hell. But I put them on with a smile even when I got blisters. That night Dad came to my room and massaged my feet and he told me that now that I have those shoes on, I know I made a mistake. If we hadn't bought them, I would have been resentful against my parents for not buying the shoes I loved. This was the lesson I had to learn on my own through the pain and the blisters. And now this lesson was forever, I couldn't unlearn it."

I yawned. "What's your point?"

"My point is," she went on patiently, "we need to do things on our own, we can go wrong but how will we grow if we aren't self-reliant. We get married as adults, so we should also make our own choices, even if they are wrong."

I lost it at that. I was the only one allowed to give her gyaan, not her.

"Yeah right." I got up from the sofa pushing her away. "And I had to marry you to know I made a mistake," I said and walked away to the bathroom oblivious to her silent tears. I didn't mean what I said, I was just provoked by her little speech, by her effort to always point out that I wasn't as independent as her, that I allowed my parents to make decisions for me.

We didn't talk for the rest of the day.

Presently, the coarse voice on the phone brought me back to the present. "Hello, sir, you there?"

"Yeah, yeah if they have tasted. We can just finalize the menu," I said.

"Sir, Meera ma'am insisted that you should choose again after tasting. So, I invite you for a lunch at our kitchen. The address is on my card. Please visit us tomorrow."

She disconnected and I was left smiling to myself.

I had to make a choice. She wanted me to choose the menu at her wedding. Is this what's called karma?

Chapter 12

Moving on

Amrita. My first meeting with her was in her noisy kitchen with her chefs around us cooking.

She briefly introduced herself and then went on to explain to me the standards of her kitchen in excruciating details in her husky voice.

I was then taken to the adjoining dining area with a five-course meal cutlery set on the table. She joined me and continued her charade. After a while I tuned out. When I was with Meera it was always both of us talking a bit followed by mute stares and comfortable silences, I wasn't used to this much information being thrown at me. Naturally I phased out and instead concentrated on the food. It was only after some time that I noticed there was some change in the surrounding; it took me a while to realize that she had stopped talking and was instead observing me eat.

"So?" she asked as soon as I met her stare.

"So what?" I asked.

"Did you hear even a word of what I said in the last many minutes?"

I smiled sheepishly.

"In my defense the food is delicious, and clearly I don't have the take or break authority here, so all the marketing is unnecessary," I replied as a matter of fact.

She looked confused and took some time to form her words. "Meera ma'am told me that you do have the authority to cancel the order."

I laughed. "Well even if I do, I am not going to as I like the food."

She gave a broad smile at that and was the first time that I noticed her effortless smile and the fact that she could have featured in a toothpaste commercial, her smile was that flawless. I had to catch myself soon enough and concentrated on the food.

"So how do you and Meera ma'am know each other?" she asked as a means to carry forward the conversation without any ulterior motive on her side.

"Didn't your Meera ma'am tell you how?" I imitated her accent.

"No," she replied with a prolonged tone to her no, like she had more to add. I just kept looking at her encouraging her to go on.

"Well in my field of work, people do talk… so I do know how you know each other," she said sheepishly.

"And yet you ask me."

She just shrugged.

"Because if what you heard is true, me sitting here doesn't make any sense right?" I put into words her thoughts.

She again replied with a prolonged, "Yes …"

"How old are you?" I asked her instead.

"Twenty-five," she replied and waited for me to go on.

"Trust me, at twenty-five I would have had the same questions as you." I got up at that and changed the topic. "So, I quite like the food and we should discuss the menu."

We spent the next hour discussing the items and the quantity and the pricing.

"So, see you at the wedding then," I said as a parting shot.

She acted a bit disturbed at that but gathered herself quickly enough. "I think we would have to discuss some more things prior to the wedding."

"You can call me anytime," I replied at that.

"Sure," she faltered. "But surely if I need to meet in person we can, right?" She looked at me expectedly and I replied with sure.

That night I had three multimedia messages from her, and I had to SMS her back saying my phone did not support MMS and she would have to mail me the said content. Within a few minutes she had mailed me pictures of some delicacies that could be replaced or used as backup.

I approved with the authority given to me.

The next day she messaged me asking if we could meet, when I asked the agenda, she had nothing concrete to say. I declined and called Meera instead. "Your caterer is irritating me with constant calls and messages." I vented as soon as she picked up.

"And you think I have the time to deal with her?" she replied in hurried tones. "I am running out of my breath here chasing the stupid event managers and arranging the right colored flowers. Palash, please deal with it." She went on.

I laughed. "And yet you hated it when everything was served to you on platter last time around. Looks like there's no pleasing you, Bridezilla ," I teased her.

"Yes I hated it," she shouted on the other side. "I might die chasing the bloody flower vendor, but my wedding will have the right shade of orange marigolds I desire."

"It's a pity Aneesh will have to marry a corpse then," I continued teasing.

"Yes, a well adorned satisfied corpse in the right colored flowers." She laughed with me. My charade had mellowed down her mood and I could hear her smiling at the other end.

"What do you want me to do Palash?" she asked next, calmly.

"Your caterer, she keeps on dropping unnecessary texts of minute details." And then I went on telling her what all Amrita had asked me to meet for.

She laughed again.

"Palash, you are not that old. I am sure you remember how it was to have a crush on someone at twenty-five. She has a crush on you and wants to meet you as much as possible. Why don't you ask her out for coffee or something?" she suggested and I went blank, so I disconnected.

I went into my shell for the next few days, in self-introspective mode as I liked to call it, with only greasy pizzas and alcohol as my companions. It is funny how alcohol acts on your brain. I had vivid dreams in those few days of that flawless smile and how it got somehow mixed with the crooked canine of Meera. I had a dream where I saw a little girl who was supposed to be my daughter and saw her grow to Amrita. In short, I had distorted visions of all the information my subconscious mind was trying to pass on to me. I decided to vent out the frustrations of my disturbed brain by playing squash. The only downside of this decision was facing Varun, but by that time I was well versed with phasing him out.

He continued his prodding into my personal life regardless as soon as we met.

"Nisha tells me Meera is getting remarried," he said, more as a statement than a question.

"I know," I replied back.

He snorted.

"Who is the guy?" he asked next

I shrugged wanting to end the discussion.

"One more life gone to waste." Varun went on regardless. "Let's see how long this one lasts."

I chose to remain silent and concentrate on my game.

"You should also think about marriage, Ash. Show Meera that you are not stuck on her, that you have moved on too." Varun went on.

"So, the reason I should marry is not because I want to but because I have to show her?" I asked sarcastically.

He shrugged as if it was the most natural thing in the world to do.

"If not now ,when?" He went on motivating me. "Look at you, you are growing old, you have grey hair."

"George Clooney has grey hair," I argued. "And the word is salt and pepper," I added with a wink. "It's supposed to be sexy."

He laughed. "Yeah so hurry before it's all salt and no pepper."

There's this thing about old friends, you might pretend that you don't care about anyone's opinion but you do.

I hit the reply button to one of the many texts sent by Amrita as soon as I was alone in the car.

The mobile buzzed back within seconds about some discussion about some random salad dressing choice

I am free now, we can meet, I texted next. We met in a cafeteria surrounded by couples and carefree teenagers. Needless to say, Amrita picked the place.

"So, I have these options of dressings, we should finalize two or three. If you can come down the kitchen, you can taste and choose…" She went on and on and I promised her that I would come down the next day even when I felt it was unnecessary.

We sat in silence for a while, interrupted by her attempts to hold the conversation with random tidbits about the food, I think I responded at the right places.

When we were about to part ways, she suggested an outing for the weekend.

"What are you doing for the weekend, I have these passes for a standup act…" she suggested.

I immediately shrunk back. I wasn't ready for it as of yet. "I don't know…" I tried to refuse but she insisted.

"I have to ask, Amrita, what about me is that interesting to you?"

She just shrugged.

"Maybe if I answer all your questions about my past with your Meera ma'am, it might satisfy your curiosity and then maybe I won't be that interesting."

She blushed at that, and I had to apologize for my directness.

"The point I am trying to make Amrita, is that I am not there yet, I am a simple divorced man who goes to work, comes home, plays video games and goes to sleep. Nothing about me is interesting."

She smiled and replied back, "What I see is a man who is big enough to do what he is doing and that's interesting to me. Yes, I see a divorced man but the kind who holds his ex-wife in his friend circle, who still cares. That is interesting. So, I ask again, I have two passes…" She left the sentence open for me to answer.

"Trust me it's all Meera, what you see is what she made me;

besides I am thirty-eight," I said instead.

"I know."

"I am too old for you Amrita." I tried again.

"And I am old enough to be a judge of that."

We went for dinner after that and parted ways to meet again the next day for a movie and the standup act over the weekend. Now that the pretenses were done with, she didn't need reasons to meet me. We met whenever either of us was free. She suggested and took me to places I would never have explored alone. For example, the concept of a day out at the mall was alien to me, but I tagged along with her as she went in shop after shop buying stuff.

"So, tell me what the trial period is?" I asked as she was checking out various cooking pots and baking pans.

She faked being hurt. "I never imagined you to be this unromantic."

I kept looking at her, waiting for an answer.

"Do I burden you?" she asked pouting for effect.

"No. I haven't had this much fun in a long time. For instance, I would never have imagined that a mall is a place to hang out."

"Where did you hang out then?" she asked next.

"We mostly met for dinners or saw movies at each other's place," I replied a bit too soon, not realizing that I was talking about Meera and me, which wasn't her question.

She just smiled.

"I can do that," she mumbled under her breath. "As for the mall, I had a shopping list, just one more thing and then we are done."

She took my hand and led me to a mobile shop. Her ease always amazed me, holding hands came naturally to her. We were not even a week old but she treated me like a buddy, not that I was complaining. I think this change was with her generation, she kept insisting that our gap wasn't much but I would be a fool to not see the differences in our outlook of life. Thirteen years for me was a huge gap, for her it wasn't even an issue and I was going with the flow.

"So, this is an Android, this is Apple which I recommend, and this is Windows, you don't want it. But all of them are what you need to live…" She went on as usual with all her descriptions and I waited for my cue to react.

"I am happy with what I have," I replied, rotating my sturdy Nokia in my hand.

"I know," she replied with a smile and proceeded to choose a suitable phone for me. I was only allowed to speak when we came out of the shop.

"This is touch screen, so you move your finger on the screen…" she started explaining and I burst out laughing.

"I know what a touch screen is, I just wanted a simple life with a simple phone. So never upgraded," I explained.

"I am sorry," she apologized. "So yeah, this is a messaging app where you can share photos, videos, audio everything. Let me send you something." And with that she clicked a selfie of the both of us and shared it with me on the app.

"You try," she ordered me and I realized she really was enjoying all the explaining.

I started exploring the app.

"Oh, she is on this too!" I exclaimed as I saw Meera's contact.

"Everyone is," Amrita replied. "Message her then," she suggested and then proceeded to take a picture of my new phone box and messaged it to her from my phone.

"See, this simple," she said with a smile.

The very next instant, Meera called.

"So, finally she convinced you to buy a new phone," she exclaimed. I didn't reply.

"Where are you?" she asked next.

"At a mall where we bought the phone," I replied.

"Is she with you?"

"Yeah."

"Oh, then I better not disturb you, bye." She was gone even before I could respond.

Amrita sat smiling at me without a word.

"What?" I had to ask.

"Did anyone tell you, your face gets so relaxed when you talk to her, like suddenly all the troubles are taken away from you?"

I didn't reply but I didn't phase out either as she continued. "All other times you have this tensed, brooding look which by the way is very sexy, but now in this window of a few seconds that you were talking with her, your guard was down. I saw the real you."

"We just go a long way back, Amrita. It's just the comfort level." I tried to defend but she smiled at me again asking me to stop.

"I am not saying that I am hurt, I am just saying I appreciate that. A while back you asked me what's the trial period, let the marriage date be the trial period. Maybe you will really know what you want when Meera ma'am gets married for real."

"It's not that." I tried defending again but wasn't allowed to continue.

"I don't want to be anyone's rebound, so the trial period is

92

the wedding which is in one week. I have been open enough to accept that I like you a lot but at the same time, I want this small window of real you, if you can take your time to get over," she concluded and got up.

I suddenly was angry.

"Amrita," I called after her and something in my eyes made her stop and listen for once. "I don't need time to get over," I said as I stood up to face her. She was almost as tall as me with her high heels so I looked straight in her kohl lined eyes as I said what needed to be said. "We were separated long back, and since then if I had my way I wouldn't have been a part of her life. It's all her. Meera made me the way I am today. Perhaps you would have hated me if you had met me years back. Whatever you find interesting about me now is what is sculpted through years of fights we both had, through her tears as I made her cry and through the efforts she put in to make me a better person. So, I am sorry but this is what you get, with Meera an integral part of me, there's no me without her and I am sorry for that as maybe it's not fair to you. But if you accept me as I am, I can promise you that there's no rebound. That ship sailed long time back. I am not in love with her any more so there's no question of rebound; there's no question of getting over."

And then I did something I would never had done otherwise, not with Meera and not before her, I hugged Amrita in public. "This is me, and this will be me with you, as I learn and grow with you," I said as I hugged her tighter, like I had seen youngsters around me do.

She hugged me back.

That was the first night we went home together for movie marathons. I showed her my favorite action movies and she showed me her favorite rom-coms and horror flicks. We had late night chat sessions and she cooked delicious food as midnight snacks. That was also the first night when Amrita and I continued chatting late in night till around three a.m. and I gently pressed the button to silence the call from Meera and let it go unanswered.

Chapter 13

Undo

I woke up the next afternoon to the dull vibration of my new phone. I started looking around and finally found the source of vibration below Amrita as she was deeply snoring oblivious to the surrounding on her stomach. I somehow managed to pull it out from under her and was shocked to see about ten missed calls from Meera. It was unusual of her to keep calling repeatedly.

I tiptoed out of the bedroom, to the living room and re-dialed Meera's number.

"Open the damn door," she shouted as soon as the phone connected. Almost on autopilot I ran to the door.

"Where were you last night?" she shouted as she entered inside and instinctively I shushed her.

She looked around and spotted the presence of Amrita in her shoes and clothes lying around the living room.

"She is sleeping," I said in hushed tones as I noticed her looking around for her.

"What happened?"

She sat down on the sofa with a thud and touched her forehead. I sat beside her waiting for her to talk.

"I should go," she said but didn't get up.

"What happened?" I asked again.

"I cannot do this," she stated.

"Cannot do what?" I asked in spite of knowing what she meant.

"This whole marriage thing," she explained and I waited for her to go on. She didn't.

"You are just nervous," I said when she didn't continue. "What's it called... pre-wedding jitters something."

"It's not that, Palash," she replied and sighed.

I waited again.

"What if marriage spoils everything that's good between us?"

"Us?" I had to ask.

"I mean Aneesh and me," she clarified and I nodded dejectedly.

"You are worrying unnecessarily," I replied.

"It did spoil everything between you and me," she stated.

"We learn from our mistakes, Meera. Everything will be okay. Aneesh is a nice guy."

"So were you. Yet I pushed you to your limits. What if Aneesh starts hating me too, post-marriage?"

"I never hated you, Meera," I said and just to placate her, placed my hands around her shoulder even as she was massaging the bridge of her nose. She did that when she was tensed.

"Everything's going to be all right," I went on, "you will see."

We both looked up with the realization of someone's presence in the room as Amrita stood at the door of the bedroom observing us.

"Everything all right?" she asked concerned, and in response Meera jerked my hand away from around her shoulder and stood up.

"Yeah, I am sorry to barge in like this, see you later."

She started walking toward the door and both Amrita and I blurted out "Wait" at the same time. Still, she turned the door knob and I reached her in two strides to turn it back again. I held her by the shoulders and brought her back to the sofa.

"Please sit," I said

"I will make some coffee," Amrita said and disappeared in the kitchen.

"So, you two hit along?" Meera teased me when Amrita was gone.

I just shrugged.

"She is a nice girl," she said next and smiled at me. "I am really happy for you," she said rubbing my thigh, and I laughed at our situation.

"Look at us Meera... life is strange. You can never imagine where you will end up."

"That's true." She sighed too. "Never imagined I will again become Meera for you. But I am glad you moved on. It lifts the guilt from my heart of getting married again."

"You shouldn't be guilty," I said.

We both sat in silence as Amrita walked in with coffee and bread with a smile.

She sat opposite us on the chair sofa and kept observing us.

"I am really sorry," Meera apologized again.

"It's okay, Meera ma'am," She replied.

"You can call me Meera," Meera replied and then looked at me, "especially now, I am sure you don't call him sir." She teased the both of us.

Amrita smiled. I couldn't help but notice the wide-eyed admiration with which she was observing both of us.

"Can I ask you something?" she said after a while and

97

Meera nodded.

"How did you manage this?" she asked and I fake put my hands in the air.

"Here she goes again," I said and winked at her.

"Manage what?" Meera asked all confused.

"Being such good friends after…" She faltered for a better word and then added, "The history."

"Why is it that strange for you?" Meera asked her instead and she again had a hard time forming words.

"I mean… how did you get over the resentment? The negativity? To be such good friends and if you are such good friends, why didn't you give a second chance to each other?" She went on blabbering.

"Who is your favorite actor?" Meera asked her and she replied with a famous young actor who was half my age.

"So, imagine you meet him, and he falls for you and proposes you and you say yes because it's obviously him! Will it be possible to adjust to his lifestyle, you know the pressure of his job and the jealousy of his beautiful lead heroines… how long would you be able to do it?"

I was listening now with curiosity as to where was the explanation going.

"I don't know," Amrita replied, "maybe I will try to be with him for a while but you are right, sooner or later one of us will give up if we had no compatibility."

"Exactly," Meera said. "Compatibility is the word. Palash and I were never compatible but that didn't make me love him any less. Will you stop loving the actor you spent your teen years pining for, after the bad marriage?" She winked at Amrita and Amrita smiled.

"You never pined for me," I interrupted

"How will you know?" Meera questioned

"C'mon." I wasn't ready to buy her argument. "She never paid any attention to me," I said to Amrita.

Meera winked at Amrita. "You are a girl; you tell me what will you do if you like a guy but the guy is too dumb to take the hint and you know it's never going to work out between the two of you?"

"Ignore him. Try to get over him," Amrita replied and Meera smiled.

"That's what I did. He was too dumb to realize I liked him. And I knew it won't work between us, we were poles apart so I tried to get over him, even left the city, but then he realized and followed me," she explained.

With every word from her, Amrita's eyes were growing wider. She asked her about my proposal next and Meera told her the whole story. She sighed at the end of it.

"But sadly, it wasn't meant to be."

Amrita sighed too.

"You don't regret it? Hate him for it?" she asked as if I wasn't in the room.

"No, I don't," she replied and then looked at me. "I am sure he doesn't either. We have come a long way to realize that marital bond is not the ultimate connection between two people. I have my girlfriends, my parents, my colleagues and I have him. When I was married to him, I was trying to search for all the above relations in him and that didn't work out. Plus, he is a foodie and I don't cook, nor do I make delicious coffee like you," she added with a smile.

Meera had a way of putting the other person at ease.

"My parents were divorced when I was around ten," Amrita said, "and they absolutely loathe each other. I spent my school year with Mom and holidays with Dad and throughout the year Mom will keep telling me how Dad spoilt her life and in holidays Dad would do the same. I ended up hating them both," she finished, emotionless. I knew her for more than a week and yet she had not told me about her family.

"So now you know why I appreciate your relationship," she concluded.

"Well, we were sane enough to not have kids, basically not fall to societal illogical reasoning that a kid will somehow set things right between us," Meera replied.

She again got up to leave. "Now I will leave you two love birds alone and get back to my marriage preparations, all the people are driving me crazy. And thanks for the coffee. I needed it."

"I will walk you to the car." I got up too.

She tried to refuse but I persisted and went down to the parking lot with her.

"You never told me that you liked me?" I said as we walked to her car.

"Why else did I marry you?" she questioned instead.

"Then why did you leave me?" I asked again. Somehow none of her answers over the many years satisfied me.

"Not again, Palash. You have something lovely waiting for you upstairs. Don't dwell in the past. You keep asking this not because we separated but because you feel I left you, that I stopped loving you. That's what hurts you. And I am telling you openly now that I never stopped loving you and never will, but that doesn't mean we have to be bound by a tag of marriage. We made each other's life hell."

"Why are you marrying Aneesh then?" I asked again.

"Because we are compatible," she replied

"But you don't love him?" I needed to know to satisfy my ego.

"He does," she replied and sat in the car.

"But you don't?" I asked again and she burst out laughing.

"Grow up Palash. Of course, I love him. Why else would I marry him?"

"But you said…" I started off but she waved me a goodbye and drove off.

When I reached back home, Amrita was cleaning up the living room. I just went in and sat on the sofa, waiting for her reaction.

"I see what you meant that day now," she said still tidying up. "Meera ma'am is just awesome. Such mellowness, I would be glad if I could be even ten percent like her."

I was thrown back to an unpleasant memory of me yelling at Meera to be at least ten percent of what Nisha was. That made me smile.

"Come here." I motioned and she walked to sit beside me as I put my arm around her. "I like you as you are, I appreciate you being so open-minded about her, but I also want to tell you that you can demand, ask me to maybe not see her this frequently or not at all, and it still will be okay. It's your right."

She smiled and snuggled close to me. "I am not stupid. You know me for two weeks and know her for two decades. I can do the math. Plus aren't we still in the trial period?" She looked up at me and winked.

"I thought we cancelled that plan. Didn't we?" I asked joining her mood.

"I would still like to wait till Meera ma'am gets married," she said and I was confused. Wait for what? We were already staying together, spending most of our time together, so what was the wait for?

"Wait for what?" I had to ask.

"For being in a relationship with you. To get serious about you," she replied nonchalantly, and I was again confused.

"So, what are we now?"

"We are friends with benefits." She winked at me. All the mumbo jumbo of youngsters confused me. I was a simple man who understood two things — being friends and being a couple. When Meera and I were friends, we had different boundaries as to when we were dating, but with the new generation all the boundaries were intermixed. Now there was platonic and just friends and dating but no future and casually dating and what not.

I got up at that.

"Let me know the status when you finalize," I said with a yawn.

"Where are we going?" she asked as I pulled her with me to lead her inside.

"Explain the friends with benefits part to me again." I winked at her and she giggled.

"I have to go," she fake protested. "The wedding is two days away. I have to go check with the groceries."

"I will come with you," I promised her. "Later," I added and she budged.

I was lying with my eyes closed after some time and Amrita asked me if I was awake. I just made a sound to indicate a yes.

"You still love her, right?" Amrita asked and I didn't want to lie. So, I didn't reply. She replied to her own question.

"I know you do. Why else would she still matter to you?"

I still didn't reply.

"You know, I wonder," she said stroking my hair as I could hear her turning to lie on her stomach and inch closer to me. I still didn't open my eyes; it was easier this way. "What is it about you? Meera ma'am said she fell for you too. So, what's your secret that made someone like Meera ma'am fall for you?"

"Say her name few more times," I teased her, Amrita was stuck on her for some reason I couldn't understand.

She hit me playfully on my shoulder.

"I am serious, what do you do really? First Meera ma'am, then me."

I laughed at that. "I doubt that, right now I think you fell more for your Meera ma'am than me. You are stuck on her."

She didn't reply for a while and I could make out that she was deep in thought.

"What if I can't do this?" she said at last and I opened my eyes to look at her.

"What if Meera ma'am is the beautiful lead heroine of my story, the one I am jealous of?" She referenced to Meera's analogy from earlier.

I pulled her closer to me to make her head rest on my shoulder.

"She is not," I lied. "We make our own story. Plus, she will be gone from our lives in a few weeks. She has Aneesh now."

"And you have me?" Amrita asked me with puppy eyes.

"After you get serious," I reminded her.

She laughed.

"Will you be able to love me as much as her?" she asked next.

I didn't want to lie any longer, so I sat up straight and looked at her even as she returned my stare with her puppy eyes. "I am thirty-eight Amrita and I was your age once, the kind of

103

love you are looking for now is something I am not capable of at this stage in life. What I am capable of is genuine concern and care for you because I really do like you a lot. And it would mean a lot to me if you think about a future with me, but if you are looking for the passionate, deeply, madly kind of love, I might not, because with my experiences I realize that it's not stable and reliable. So really, you have all right to walk out if we aren't on the same page."

Her eyes welled up at that and I was genuinely sorry for her. I had to be honest.

"I am sorry," I said as I again pulled her to me.

"It's okay," she said, trying to hold back tears. "My fault, I didn't meet you earlier." She smiled at me.

"I want to be with you," she said next.

"I want you to want to be with me too," I replied, and she laughed a bit at my tongue twister.

"But you have already loved her passionately and you cannot love me the same way again. It's done for!" She used a pronoun for Meera too.

I then understood what Meera meant when she said that she loved Aneesh, as I replied with "but I do love you."

There comes a stage in Solitaire when you think you are winning and in that confidence you unravel another set of cards, which creates a huge mess and then you aren't closer to the end but are instead struggling with the new cards dealt. Nothing fits and the only option is to press the undo button to put the new cards back and strategize.

Life unfortunately doesn't have an undo button.

Chapter 14

Queen of Hearts

"Please stay," I said. It wasthe night before her big day. Amrita and I had just finished dinner that she had expertly cooked and was picking her stuff to leave.

"Really can't, tomorrow is the day! I have to get up early and reach the venue to make sure everything is on time."

"I will drop you in the morning," I suggested, anything to make her stay.

"I will be getting up at four, Palash. You have a good night's sleep and we will meet at the venue," she persisted and reached the door

I didn't tell her that I didn't want to be alone, that I would rather be with her for few hours than look ahead to a sleepless night. She left nonetheless and I was left alone with my thoughts and alcohol. Before I could put my thoughts into action, Amrita returned and walked straight to the fridge to take out all the bottles of alcohol with her.

"I am sorry. I really need to go," she said pecking my cheek. "But I also want you to be sober tomorrow."

I stood there without any reaction and she was gone.

With nothing else to do, I was back to playing Solitaire, this time on my new smartphone. Minutes turned to hours even as the master that I was failed to finish.

Don't. I sent a single word of text to Meera around

midnight hoping it would convey all that I wanted to say to her.

Go to sleep, she replied back.

Can't. Why are you awake? I wrote.

Because it's my wedding and I am too anxious to sleep. Trying, she replied with an emoticon.

Shall I come over? I texted next, really hoping to and she replied with a, *Lol and Gn,* leaving me alone yet again.

Everything between us was said and done for. There was nothing else that could change things between us and I trying relentlessly wasn't going to help either. Still, I didn't give up. I wasn't even sure what kept twisting my heart more; the fact that she had moved on for real with someone who could give her what I couldn't, or the fact that she had moved on for real and I hadn't. Both the scenarios made me the loser. After spending the whole night floating in and out of sleep, it was time to put on the mask and masquerade with pride as I played the perfect host at the wedding.

It was show time.

Each and every detail of the wedding venue had her name written all over it. It was her day, the way she always wanted. I tried remaining out of her vision and of her relatives as I mingled with people on the groom's side, yet making sure she wasn't out of my sight even for once. She looked radiant and happy and what I saw was two people in love with each other tying the knot. Aneesh had all his attention on her and things sailed smoothly and perfectly. She was the planner after all. I didn't realize that Amrita was now standing beside me, even she had changed into festive clothes. I didn't notice her as I was lost in yet another reverie of our wedding.

I was too conscious of everyone around me, Aneesh looked comfortable, and I wasn't.

I was too aware of everyone around me, Aneesh had eyes just for her. Some of my relatives had passed a loose comment about us not getting any dowry and my mother had supported the claim. Meera had looked at me for support and I ignored the comment.

"You aren't going to say anything?" she had whispered to me and I had replied with "They are just pulling your leg; you don't need to take it seriously. That's what happens at weddings."

She had not spoken a word till the end of the ceremony as she was bombarded with cruel jokes from my side of the family throughout the day. Now that I looked back, I am surprised that she didn't leave me that day itself!

Everything of the wedding brought back a memory of the day I let it go all wrong to please my family. The day I let us grow apart. She never got over her resentment of that day and I worsened it with my inaction. I was jolted back to present by a familiar voice. "Shameless some people are!" Amrita and I turned back together to see Varun sneering at Meera.

I let out a sigh. "Not the time, not the place."

"Look at her all decked up to ruin another life." He went regardless.

Amrita looked at me and I had to introduce. I said their respective names.

Before Varun could even mutter a hi toward Amrita as he stood with his best fake smile, Amrita blurted out, "Oh so you are the Tybalt to this Romeo and Juliet."

"The what?" Varun replied flabbergasted.

"Too high brow for you?" She frowned and gave him a fake smile. "Can't say it was nice to meet you."

For once in his life Varun was speechless. He looked at me,

but I was speechless too.

He patted me on the shoulder, his eyes saying all that he didn't about my choice of women and was about to leave before Amrita called after him. "And Varun, it's wiser to keep your mouth shut when you have nothing nice to say." He was about to reply but decided against it and was gone. I looked at Amrita and she had a complacent smile playing on her lips.

"What was this?" I had to ask.

"What?" she questioned back. "Don't tell me, you are offended! He deserved what he got."

"Yeah, but like you said, it's wiser to be silent when you have nothing nice to say."

I repeated her words.

"Nothing nice to say about nice people, not jerks," Amrita replied. She had a fair idea of the kind of person Varun was from the frequent late night chats we had but I never expected her to be so vocal about it.

"You know what happens if you keep your mouth shut with jerks?" She asked a rhetorical question and then pointed at Meera. "That happens."

I didn't know how to respond so I kept looking at her. The sun was in her eyes and she squinted up to look at me. "I am not her Palash. Not the suffer in silence types. I am what you see and that's what you get. I command respect, if you can't deal with it, your loss," she concluded.

Meera always maintained a dignified silence around Varun. None of his jabs reached her as she refused to be dragged down to his level. Amrita had made her stand clear.

"So that's one friend less from my life," I concluded.

"Don't be silly. He is your buddy, you maintain your friendship, just don't expect me to be cordial toward him." She had a distinct category for all her relations and I suddenly started respecting her clarity and segregation. She refused to be victimized. We continued observing the bride and groom as the rituals ended and people made a beeline to congratulate the couple.

"Are we going up the stage?" she asked next.

"Yeah. Why not?"

"I meant 'we'," she clarified.

In return I took her hand in mine and started walking toward the stage. She was smiling when I looked at her with a side glance. We had to join the long queue and wait patiently.

Amrita looked up at me and kept observing me for a while as I had my whole attention on the stage.

"What?" I had to ask when she didn't stop.

"I am just wondering…" she said but didn't explain what.

I just gestured her to go on.

"…about how someone can love someone so much."

I had no answer.

"How do you do that, Palash? Stand here with these controlled emotions," she asked next and kept looking at me.

"Not the time, not the place." I repeated what I said earlier as the people ahead of us turned back interested in our conversation.

Amrita bit her tongue. I didn't reply to her but her questions made me think. How was I able to stand there emotionless when the only thing I wanted to do was run to the stage, punch Aneesh and pull Meera away for me. What was holding me back? I kept asking myself as I saw Meera brush something away from Aneesh's face that sent a sharp pang to my heart. It was her, holding me back, keeping me sane. The look on her face that radiated complacency, that showed she was finally at peace with herself. And even as I hated the man who made her feel this way, I accepted that the hatred sprung from jealousy of not being the one. He mattered to her and that itself made him a friend not a foe. We kept moving ahead in the queue, with Amrita by my side and my thoughts getting sorted, the haze lifting, the cards setting in order. The queen of hearts and her king of hearts were on the stage, inseparable, wherever they would move henceforth would be together as they matched the suits. I was just a King of Spades in the story. Meera had tried being with me, but that was short-lived as we didn't belong together, there wasn't a movement possible together. She had found her own column and would soon be sorted. I had to let go of her to find my own Queen of Spades; I could not remain attached to the Queen of Hearts as that would mean mess for both of us.

We reached the stage and Aneesh hugged me as I congratulated him.

"Thanks for coming," he said, "it means a lot to both of us."

Meera smiled at me and I noticed that she was teary-eyed as she sniffled, her smile still intact.

"Come here," she said and hugged me too, her tears reflected in my eyes but she gathered herself and looked at Amrita with a huge smile and muttered a thanks to her which I didn't understand. "Don't be a fool and let this one go," she told me sternly. We posed for photos and then Amrita and I climbed down the stage.

If I had to draw an analogy with a movie plot, this would be the intermission.

But I started this with the analogy of the game of Solitaire so let me say the Queen of Hearts was back with her King and her deck was safely sorted together. What was left was me out there with a lot of mess to clear, my Queen by my side.

Chapter 15

Lost

It had been a month since she married, and I won't say that I was tracking her, but somehow, I knew she was on her honeymoon in Fiji. I didn't even know where that was on the map. Amrita showed me pictures of a happy her with a happy him, smiling at the camera.

"How do you have them?" I asked as she sat next to me on the bed scrolling through image after image of a radiant, tanned Meera next to a handsome Aneesh. I had never met Aneesh in a relaxed setting so it was my first time seeing him in casuals and tee shirts.

"Aneesh sir is a catch," Amrita remarked as she kept on scrolling and I had to act hurt.

I cleared my throat and looked at her. She smiled, still scrolling when she noticed me looking at her.

"Oh, c'mon! He is. Just look at the pictures! He is handsome, caring and he loves her so much. What more can a girl ask for?"

She wouldn't stop scrolling and I couldn't stop looking but what I was seeing was different from what Amrita was. I saw Meera; it was like ten years were taken off her as she stood confidently beside her new husband smiling at the camera. She could give any runaway model a run for her money. And I had let her go. No, in fact I had been offered that and I twisted it into something unrecognizable and then threw it away. I was thrown into another reverie where she and I argued over her clothes.

"Why do you wear such ill-fitting clothes?" I had asked her after a bowling evening with Varun and Nisha some months after our marriage. Nisha was in a tee and jeans and Meera was in some flowy thing she called something.

"Coz that's what fits!" she had shouted back, obviously angry at my question.

"That's why I say no to take-aways," I replied back and she had thrown her hands in air in frustration.

"Seriously Palash? Are you like telling me right now that how I look embarrasses you?"

I had to retract before I could cause irreparable damage so I apologized and covered it up with mushy, romantic stuff. She cried regardless.

"If only I was not crying all the time or fighting with you all the time, I would actually have the mental state to pay attention to myself," she had accused me.

"If you would pay attention to yourself, maybe you won't fight all the time," I had replied.

Amrita pulled me back from that memory by moving on to the next image where Meera stood on a beach in a bikini with sun glasses over her head and a sarong tied around her waist. Her elbow was resting on a shirtless Aneesh's shoulder.

"Wow," Amrita said even before I could say a thing. "I take my words back. They are made for each other."

I had enough as I closed the flap of the laptop.

"How do you even see them? She shared it with you?" I asked.

"Oh no. I follow Aneesh sir on his Instagram."

I didn't have the energy to ask what that was.

She tried opening the laptop again but I stopped her. "Let's just not," I said and this time she looked at me strange.

"Are you like affected by this?"

She pointed at the laptop and I had to lie with, "Of course, not."

She saw through it. "I thought you said you were ready?" She accused me and I hated the tone, the same tone that Meera used when I messed up. It made me feel guilty and it made me feel little. It pushed me into a defensive zone. Like when I was a kid and Dad used that tone and I had to defend myself from being bashed up. Childhood fears had carried to adulthood and now when I was accused, I immediately reacted by blaming the other person so that I could go scot-free.

"You said the marriage was the trial period? So where are we now, what about your readiness?" I asked back in the same tone as if the question was logical.

"I am here. Am I not?" she questioned back.

"As what?" I questioned again. "You have all that stupid levels of friends and benefits and what not. How do I know I am not just an escort to you?"

I didn't know why I was angry or that why was I taking it out on Amrita.

She dropped her jaw at that and then got up to get dressed and left. I didn't stop her. My mobile buzzed as soon as I heard the door close after her.

It was a message from Amrita. *I will be waiting for an apology if and when you are ready.*

I threw the mobile on the bed in rage. I really had to figure out why I was this angry. I went back to the laptop Amrita left and scrolled through all the images again and then for good measure threw the laptop too!

It took me few days to come back to sanity and Amrita didn't call me or message me for those few days. It was like she didn't exist.

I went to her kitchen when I was stable enough.

"You cannot show up at my workplace unannounced. We will talk later," she said as soon as she saw me and ushered me out.

"I came here to apologize."

"Accepted," she said and continued ushering me out.

"Accepted the apology or the fact that I came here to apologize?" I asked.

"Both," she said with a smile and again repeated that she would meet me in evening.

"Come home," I requested, although I knew her answer.

She declined. "Not sure if I will do that again, Palash. You don't have the maturity to understand me and I cannot fall down to your level."

I was angry again, somehow the fact that girls used the tone of a mother in a fight really pissed me off.

"If you think I am not capable of you, why meet me at all?"

"Because I am stupid enough to still love you," she said and started crying. Another thing I hated.

I apologized harder for what I said that morning and then gave her the brochures I brought with me.

"You pick a place we will go for a vacation."

She nodded her head in denial.

"Just because she is on her honeymoon?" she asked me.

"No, because you couldn't stop looking at her pictures, I figured you need a vacation too," I lied.

"I am not a kid so please don't treat me like one. I was

excited for them, not jealous," she replied

"Regardless, shall we go for a vacation?"

She declined again. Somehow, I had managed to push the second female who showed some interest in me away too.

I stood there without having anything else to carry forward the conversation.

"About the trial period, I think it's over. And we are done. I don't think you are ready to move on and more than me you need to stop lying to yourself and stop pretending that she doesn't matter to you. Only then could you really move on. "

"You know that's not true," I argued.

"Maybe it's not, but I cannot stay here with the 'her' between us forever."

"You always knew I had a past, it's not like she cropped up just yesterday."

"I did and I also thought I had the maturity to handle it, I can handle a past relationship, Palash, but I cannot handle a present. The problem with you is that she is your present."

I shrugged and walked away with no answer and no motivation to fight.

Chapter 16

The King of Hearts

With Amrita gone, I was back to my earlier life of work, squash and Solitaire. The uncomplicated existence was back with the only change being the smartphone. It was indeed comfortable and a blessing for a loner like me. Solitaire was comfortable on the phone too and yes; I was tracking her on Instagram. She was back from Fiji and was in India to enjoy her vacations before flying to U.S.A. forever. I waited for her to call, for her to remember that I existed.

And she did as she called me a few days after coming back and invited me and Amrita for dinner.

"I am afraid, she isn't with me anymore," I said over the phone, and I could hear her silent scream as she tried too hard to not overreact.

"You can freak out," I reminded her but perhaps something in my voice made her not pull my leg this time around.

"So is the invitation still valid?" I asked and she immediately replied with yes.

"You sure it won't be uncomfortable?" I had to be sure.

"Don't be silly," she reprimanded me and that's how I landed up in their temporary flat for dinner amidst flowers, decaying bouquets, matching suitcases and a radiant Aneesh and Meera. I needed new adjectives to define her. Since her marriage, I was falling short of words to describe her happiness

116

and I was a crappy person who didn't believe in the concept of 'I would be happy for you irrespective of you being mine or not'. I wanted her to be mine. The fact that she wasn't was breaking me inside. I had taken the high road of attending her marriage and being there for her, but Amrita had made me realize that I did all that in a hope that she would return, in a tiny little expectation that Aneesh won't turn up at the marriage and I would be there for her; the only glitch being I wasn't when she needed me and now she didn't need me anymore.

Aneesh invited me in and I walked in with a bottle of wine and flowers for her.

"This was unnecessary," Meera said formally as she took them from me. I could see the concern in her eyes for me and the unsaid question asking what went wrong, how I screwed up again.

"I will take care of them," Aneesh said, taking the flowers from her. "You make sure he is comfortable." He gave us the privacy where she could freak out.

"What happened?" she asked as soon as Aneesh was out of sight.

"She didn't appreciate me being hung up on you." I told the truth.

"And why are you?" She almost shouted but then restrained herself, peeking inside for Aneesh who I was sure was taking all the time to give us the time to have this conversation.

"Because I am not you," I hissed at her. "I wasn't brought up with the approach of giving up on marriages. In my family everybody who married, stayed married. I cannot keep jumping like you."

"Stayed married with the thought of killing each other every day. Don't give me this crap, Palash, after all this time," she said.

"You asked."

"So, you come here to tell me that you were fooling me all these years, since we separated?" she accused with a deep-rooted resentment in her voice that I had never seen her use.

"Say whatever you want Meera. But I cannot play your little game anymore. We were married and I cannot act like that was nothing and suddenly we are friends."

"What are you angry at Palash?" she asked me like my shrink and it provoked me further. I was angry at her for moving on, for not realizing that I always wanted a second chance, that it was the only reason for being in touch with her all these years to accept that I screwed up first time around and now I needed another chance to prove myself to her. That all the events of past, Amrita, her wedding, me meeting her for dinners was a haze now. The only clear memory I had was of her in that stupid dress at the airport in her hometown and smiling at me, faking anger and me standing in front of her asking her to marry me. I wanted a restart from there. Nothing else mattered. I was angry at her inability to see my anguish. I was angry at her selfishness. And I said that.

"I am angry that I fell hopelessly in love with a selfish person like you who sees nothing beyond her own needs."

She exhaled forcefully at that to regain her composure. "I am married, Palash, to him," she pointed at the kitchen, "and you are standing here like some psycho professing your twisted form of love for me, think about who really is selfish here."

She turned her back to me to go inside indicating that the conversation was over.

Aneesh stepped out of the kitchen with the flowers in a pot and a smile on his face. He figured that something was wrong with us as I stood in the middle of the room and Meera was going inside.

"Have a seat, please," he said to me and before I could move Meera replied for me.

"Actually, he is leaving."

I just stood there and Aneesh sighed.

"No, he is not," he replied for both of us. "We invited him, Meera, and this is our house where our guests will be treated with respect whatever the problem is. We are going to sit and eat together and talk about whatever has both of you fuming." He sat on the dining chair for effect and then ordered both of us. "So, I say again, sit." And like two children we did sit. There was something about the voice of reason that made dramatic people listen. Aneesh was the voice of reason.

We continued eating in silence and making small talk. I couldn't help observing both of them together. They didn't need words to converse. He looked at her, she got the message and reacted accordingly. There was a lot of talking through the eyes which I didn't understand. What I did understand was that I was a mute spectator to how beautiful a marriage could be when both partners were equally involved.

"Can you please make some coffee for us?" Aneesh asked Meera at the end of the quiet dinner, and she got up as I sniffled a laugh.

"I will pass, if she is making the coffee." I winked at her as my way of apologizing for my earlier behavior.

Aneesh laughed, a good-hearted, clear laughter with his head up in the air.

"I totally agree there," he replied, "but don't worry we have a coffee maker. I bought it right after the first coffee she made." He winked at her too and she responded by playfully hitting

119

him.

Aneesh looked at me as soon as she entered the kitchen and was out of hearing shot.

"May I say something to you, Palash, if you allow me?" He asked for my consent and I had to play a good guest so I nodded.

"I always knew what I was getting into," he went on. "When I first met her, I knew she was still in love with you. And all I wanted was to somehow get the both of you together. I saw it as a wasted opportunity, how both of you let go of something which could have been very beautiful." He leaned me as he said the next part. "But I also know and even you do toward how stubborn she is. She was burnt with you and I am not blaming you at all. I am a big believer of it takes two to tango philosophy. Call it karma or whatever but maybe you both weren't meant to be. And she knows that. But she genuinely cares for you and I can live with that. I can even live with the fact that a part of her will always be in love with you. But she has moved on, I would have been a fool to marry her if she hadn't. And I can also see that you haven't moved on." He took a pause waiting for me to react, but I had nothing to say, nothing to him at least.

He sighed and went on. "Everyone deserves a second chance. You do too. If you look beyond your stubbornness to get her. Because trust me, I am not letting her go without a fight. You are important to her and so by extension you are important to me. You are family, if you want to be. You are always welcome in this house, Palash, only you have to realize that she is gone and happy and that's what you should wish for family. Happiness. That's what I wish for you. Give me a chance to prove every word I said to you. What you both have is something very beautiful which does not need a validation of marriage, don't let go of that, please, for her sake, because I can see how you matter to her. Don't become her past, Palash. Don't give her a reason to give up on you, to throw you away from her life. You know that you both need each other as you both share something which I can never be to her. Think about it."

He wrapped up as he could hear Meera walking back.

"What are you guys whispering about?" she asked and Aneesh brushed her off .

"About who will carry whom to hospital after the coffee," he joked and she acted hurt.

"Cut it out, Aneesh," she said and sat next to him as Aneesh took the tray without her asking him to and served the coffee for us.

I was thrown back to another reverie of my mother reprimanding Meera for expecting me to serve in front of Varun and Nisha. Again, it was a few months after the marriage and we had invited both of them for dinner. Meera was already tired after a hard day's work and still she went ahead with the plan. I had called my mother for help. Meera struggled with the cooking and then she called for me to start serving the food on the table. Varun sent Nisha and my mother turned her nose up. "This is the problem with the working types, they always want to turn the husbands into servants," she had said, Varun had laughed and Meera had ignored and as usual I had not stood up for her.

When the topic came up after Varun and Nisha left, I defended my mother by saying that I did help in her absence but Meera had to learn to not assign chores to me in presence of my mother to respect her thinking and feelings for me.

"That's the problem, Palash, with you, some or the other

pretense is always up. You cannot be you ever and I cannot be me. We just keep pretending. Keep living for everyone else but us," she had said which had led to another fight and another night of her sleeping on the sofa. I always went into a shell after every fight and resurfaced only when she had forgotten. She pleaded with me to not act distant but I did to reinforce my displeasure.

I was again pulled back from this memory with Aneesh offering the cup to me.

"All the best," he said and again Meera playfully hit him.

"I have no shame in admitting that I am no good at cooking," Meera said and Aneesh smiled at her. "I know that and no one is expecting you to cook. As long as you don't expect me to do things I hate."

"Like what?" she asked

"Like giving up on people who matter?" he said and held her stare. She looked away. They again had some conversation with their eyes and Meera looked at me with a smile. "I am sorry Palash for whatever I said earlier. But it's your fault too…" she tried going on but Aneesh interrupted.

"I think I am sorry is enough." He smiled at her, took her hand and kissed the back of her hand.

"I am sorry too," I said on autopilot.

Aneesh sat back at that, like he had achieved what he set out to achieve and I kept sipping on the coffee looking at both of them, looking at what could have been and looking at the person I could have been.

"So, what happened to Amrita?" he asked me now, "if I may ask."

"Like always, I screwed up," I replied in all honesty.

"Not necessarily," the love guru said. "If you really want

her back you just need a gesture."

I laughed at that. "Seriously, Aneesh, I am all ears! Just let me know what grand gesture will make her come back," I said and I knew he got what I meant.

He laughed too. "Step one, make sure she is not really gone." He raised his hand which was intertwined with Meera's to kiss it again and pass on the message that Meera was. "If not, you need a grand gesture to prove that you are there for her and for future remember that it's the small things that matter in any relationship. A coffee maker, a cook and smiling to a tasteless meal are small prices to pay for a happy relationship." He winked at me.

I sighed and got up to leave at that. "It's the generation, Aneesh, your generation is brought up after globalization. I respect the romanticism of your generation. We were brought up with a rigid mind set and I am still trying to figure out how many adjustments I do need as a person."

He smiled and got up too. "There are just five years between us, Palash, not really a generation gap and I cannot speak about the globalization but yes, I grew up with an alcoholic, abusive father and that made me realize what I really don't want to be. It's only about the choices you make."

For once I had no answer. Varun and I were of the same generation and I was frequently amazed by his repressiveness, then there was Aneesh who made me feel regressive. I didn't know where the buck stopped. What I did know was that I stood at the marriage with the realization that my Queen of Hearts was gone, and I was left behind to cope with the mess left on the screen with my Queen of Spades or whatever who for now was in some other corner, but I had a chance of being with her again. Now as I exited their apartment with a smiling Aneesh shaking my hand and Meera standing with her hand around his waist, waving a goodbye at me; I realized that I wasn't left behind. The Queen of Hearts was with her king who deserved her in every sense of the word. There's was a different world which thrived on emotions, love, grand gestures, all that Meera always wanted. Aneesh really was the king of hearts who carried his heart on his sleeve, who didn't shy away from expressing his emotions who didn't care for anyone except his woman. I was not Aneesh and that was fine. Maybe my Queen of Spades will understand that, will understand that I wasn't about words and I wasn't about sharing but that didn't mean that I didn't care, that I didn't love. Meera and I not working out didn't make me a bad person, it just proved that we weren't meant for each other.

And that was fine.

Everything was fine.

If only, my Queen of Spades will have me again. Will accept me as I was.

Chapter 17

Gestures

Life happens and keeps happening to you irrespective of you striving for it or not. Irrespective of you wanting it to happen or not. You cannot just declare that you are done. It doesn't work that way. Similarly, it doesn't work if you wait for things to happen to you. You cannot stop one aspect of your life to focus on other. Cannot keep waiting. I didn't stop living because Meera was married now. I didn't stop working because I had a crappy personal life. It went on, I found hobbies, I found solace in many other things, more importantly I survived, I moved on.

It's like Solitaire, the cards will keep coming. The only logical next step after clearing the mess on the screen is dealing a new set. There's no other way if one has to move on or move ahead. The message is, 'Deal with the mess and move on'. I had waited a lot to clear the mess before I realized that the mess was all in my head. I was stalling, afraid to move on thereby delaying the road to the end.

Meera was with Aneesh in the U.S. We gradually lost touch, both realizing that when we did meet again it would be like we never separated. Both realizing that we were just a phone call away if need be and both knowing that we were past the stage of passionate over the top love for each other. It was replaced with a genuine concern for other.

And this is where I started, didn't I? With a claim that we

weren't in love with each other. We weren't any more. Not the form of love that is saleable anyway. So, I ask again, does such a story deserve a telling? A story without sudden plot twists, no drama and no surprises. Did I disappoint you so far?

I didn't disappoint myself at least. I started out as a man too sure of my growth as a person, proud enough to declare that I wasn't in love with her. I was shown the mirror by a much younger person, Amrita, who made me realize that I was a liar. Now I stand at a place where I make the same claim, this time with a humility to accept that I was beyond passion, beyond stubbornness with a realization that Aneesh is the best person for her. He can be her pronoun and I could be her past. I could live with that without jealousy. Because frankly jealousy comes when there is competition. There was no competition here. You cannot compare apples to oranges, you cannot compare Hearts to Spades. That's the whole gist and this is what I claim as growth.

My Bildungsroman.

My story of what happens after happily ever after.

I have no life lessons to share here. Just the fact that there were once two people madly in love with each other, who got married and decided to spend the rest of their lives with each other but then they parted ways not by a blow of fate but by their own misgivings. And now they are not together. This will be the gist if someone asks you what the story is all about. You can reply with this, say it's a crap story. I don't care. What I do care about is the man I see looking back at me when I see the mirror. A man who doesn't escape his troubles with Solitaire, but a man who faces life head on. Who right now is standing in his best clothes in front of the mirror, combing the salt and pepper hair and ensuring the ring is safe in his pocket as he plans to take matters in his own hands and go for the girl who made him happy when he thought there was no happily ever after. A girl who brought some fun back to his life when he was living trapped in the past, believing that he could spend his whole life there. That girl deserved a happy ending too. I deserved a happy ending too. I had to make sure that next time she professed her love for me it would be without tears, without the hopelessness.

We needed hope.

We needed a happily ever after.

We needed to belong.

We all do.

Beyond the everyday chores that we try to convince ourselves are very important, beyond the money that we try to accumulate, we are humans who need to belong. And both Amrita and I deserved it. I needed to replace the last memory of Amrita crying and saying that she was still in love with me to a memory where she would always be smiling and grow old with me.

I don't think it was too much to ask out of my life. I took the car out of the parking to pick her up from outside the kitchen as decided. She had agreed to meet me and as Aneesh said, I just needed a gesture.

I was ready to take a plunge. It's like Solitaire, you feel the rush when you know there's just one suit out in the open and only the twos and fives to collect and drag below the neatly stacked kings, queens and jacks. You have it under control and you know it. You just feel it. That was the rush I felt as I reached closer to her place.

Except...

Life isn't a game of Solitaire. I cannot draw parallels. Life

127

isn't that simple.

I could see Amrita standing in her trademark jeans and black tee waiting for me and I took a turn to meet her with only one thought on my mind. A gesture. I again patted the ring in my pocket. Just a gesture.

She smiled at me as I slammed the brakes and opened the car door for her.

"I am sorry for whatever I put you through," I said

"Accepted," she replied with a smile.

"Accepted the apology or the fact that I put you through a lot?" I asked

"Both."

"So where do you want to go?" I asked next.

"Nowhere," she replied. Her being monosyllabic made me realize that it wasn't going to be easy. It wasn't going to be as simple as stacking twos and threes.

I parked in a safe parking spot and turned to her.

"So, we talk here," I said and she just shrugged.

I sighed as I realized that the gesture in my pocket was useless now. It would be like the holiday brochures. I also realized that it wasn't me she was interested in right then but the fact that she sat in the car with me was the second chance I was getting, one that I never got with Meera. I couldn't screw this one up. I couldn't speak about myself because none of the explanations I would give now for my crappy behavior would make her stay. The only thing that would make her stay was the assurance that I would be there for her, that I belonged to her.

I am sure you caught the pattern here. There is a reason pronouns are pronouns. I won't say they are replaceable. Meera still was my pronoun but now in that instance Amrita was too. It was all about her.

And I realized that.

"I will not explain my behavior in the past to you Amrita, because all I say will sound like excuses. But what I will say is what you deserve in a person and that's unconditional love and care. There isn't a comparison here, but you need to pull both Meera and I down from the pedestal you have placed us on. We both are humans who erred but who also learnt from our mistakes. I am not promising you that I will not err in future. I am as much a human as you are, so obviously I will keep on screwing up and you will too, but what matters is; will we both give each other second chances? Will we both be ready to commit to our future together? If we both are on the same page on this, I think I am here for you."

She laughed for what seemed an eternity.

"That's the most unromantic proposal ever, Palash."

I had no words. I was hurt and that reflected on my face.

She quickly apologized. "I am not trying to put you down dear, please know this. I might use this tone which makes you feel so, but that's only because I am disappointed in you and that's fair. We only get disappointed in people we expect from. It's an indication that I still am here, in this relationship that I still care."

I nodded. I had hated Meera using this tone and always took it as her way of putting me down to have the upper hand. I had never seen this side of the argument and I needed to know the right way to respond. To not retaliate.

"How am I supposed to react to this, Amrita? Because frankly I feel little when you laugh at me." I decided to have the conversation I never had with Meera.

Amrita turned to me and cupped my face, to reverse all the feeling of being unloved to a deep satisfaction of being important. I leaned against her palm.

"You react by saying exactly what you feel, because I may not realize that I make you feel this way."

I nodded.

"So, start again." She smiled.

"With what?" I had to ask

"With a romantic proposal," she suggested.

"I don't know what to say," I confessed.

"What did you say to Meera at the airport all those years back?"

I sighed again. "Amrita, I am not the same person now."

She smiled. "Relationships don't work on terms and conditions, Palash. You sitting here with me is proof enough for me that you care, that you want this as much as me. Just that I would have loved to hear it out loud."

"Fair enough," I replied. "Years back I stood at an airport in an unknown city in front of a girl I madly loved, and I said some things to her and now I am tongue tied because I feel anything I say now will sound fake in front of what I said then. Like I am not allowed to feel those emotions again, that I am an imposter if I now say that I feel the same passion for you. Except that I am not. I should be allowed to again, stand in front of you and confess my love for you without the fear of being laughed at or being thought of as a cheater. And I am taking this chance Amrita, of being laughed at for you. Of sitting here with you at thirty-nine years of age but still feeling the butterflies in my stomach that I felt then. Only because I am sure you are the one. I maybe older in age but you are the mature one. You are the one who showed me that I was allowed to live again... I was allowed to love again... that..."

She stopped me before I could go on.

"You are allowed everything, Palash. It's your life and you shouldn't be ashamed of any part of it."

"Thanks," I murmured.

Both of us didn't say anything for a long time. The ring was like a huge rock in my pocket but I knew now wasn't the time. A grand gesture was not something that worked always. It did for the suits of Hearts not for us practical Spades. For us honesty and loyalty worked.

"So, what do you say?" I asked Amrita

"Take me home," she replied.

The final stack was back in the deck again.

The screen was clear.

Chapter 18

Beyond the ever after…

"I am going to throw your phone away; what kind of person calls you at such an early hour!" Amrita mumbled all disturbed as she adjusted her blanket and kept turning in bed to find a comfortable position again. She hated being disturbed from her lovely sleep. I checked my mobile, it was Meera's one word SMS, *Thank you,* sent from across the hall, from the spare bedroom.

A fortnight earlier I had woken up to the vibration of my phone in a similar way. "Please pick it up," I had heard Amrita mumble. She wasn't an early riser and hated to be awakened by any external disturbances.

"I get grumpy throughout the day if I don't get up on my own," was her explanation always. And after she woke up, she needed a cup of espresso right away which yours truly provided. Only after that she would be in a state to be approachable. As someone said to me years back, small prices to pay for a happy relationship. Once she took charge after the caffeine kicked in, she was the boss.

I tiptoed out of the room and pressed the accept button. Meera was on the other side shrieking in an excited tone.

"Guess what? We are coming back. Aneesh's contract expired and we decided to shift base back to India. Isn't that cool?"

I mumbled back with, "Hi... how are you?"

"I am great, Palash. I just wanted to tell you as soon as we finalized. We fly back this weekend," she went on.

"That's great. I look forward to meeting you," I said next.

"Of course, you do! I will call you once we land and check in a hotel."

"Why hotel?"

"Our place has been locked for three years, of course Aneesh sent someone to clean but I need room service after the long flight," she explained and I smiled.

"What you need is a nice comfortable bed to sleep. I will arrange your pick-up, you drive straight home," I ordered.

"No, Palash, that won't be necessary..." she tried to argue but I insisted and that's how she landed up that weekend in the spare bedroom.

I replied saying, "Go to sleep." And then put the phone on silent to again go back to sleep. I had sent the driver to pick them up with a spare key. I was yet to see her and all I wanted was to get up and walk across the room, it had been too long since I saw her last but I resisted and waited for a decent hour. After drifting in and out of sleep for couple of hours, I woke up and walked to the kitchen for the daily routine of brewing the espresso for Amrita. This was the only time I entered the kitchen, then it was Amrita's domain. I was busy with the daily routine when Aneesh greeted me with a good morning.

"Did I wake you up?" I had to ask.

"No... no... The time difference screws up the body clock. Can I get one too?" he asked pointing at the coffee.

I passed a cup to him and that gave me the time to observe him. He looked a lot mature than the last time I saw him and a lot fitter too.

He took a sip of coffee and sighed. "Thanks for doing this. Nothing beats the homely atmosphere after a long flight."

"My pleasure." I maintained the formality.

He smiled at that. "When did we meet last?"

"Don't know. Three years, Four..." I tried to calculate.

"Time really flies, I am married for three years. Wow," he said more to himself than me.

I just smiled.

"You guys didn't miss home?"

"Home is where the heart is," the King of Hearts replied and I smiled again. "No, frankly, I didn't. Meera did, I think initially; then life happened, she got a job, we both got busy... but she did keep waiting for the marriage invite from you to get a chance to come home I guess."

I laughed at that.

"That never came," he concluded.

"Well... what can I say, we both are happy with things as they are. The thought of marriage never crossed our minds." I decided to be honest.

"Fair enough," he replied and picked his cup up. "You mind if I take this back to the room. I am sure Meera will appreciate some decaf too."

I shrugged.

"See you after we freshen up," he said as a parting shot and went to his room.

And I went back to Amrita with the cup of coffee and like every day I was on the laptop catching up on work as she snored lightly besides me. She woke up an hour later and like every day searched for the cup of coffee on the bedside table with her eyes still half closed.

"They reached?" she asked when she was awake and I

134

nodded.

"I should make some breakfast," she said next and got up from the bed.

"Relax, I think they are still asleep."

"You met?"

"Aneesh not Meera," I replied without looking up from the laptop.

An hour later we were at the breakfast table.

"Should we wake them up?" Amrita asked as both our guests were still asleep.

"I don't think so," I replied and we continued eating.

Aneesh stepped out a few minutes later. He had taken a bath and changed since I saw him in morning.

"I am sorry," he apologized to the room. "Meera will be here soon," he added and greeted Amrita with a bear hug to sit beside me on the table.

"Amrita, thanks for having us," he said to her.

She replied with, "It's my pleasure, Aneesh sir."

"I think you can drop the sir now." He winked at her, and she blushed.

"Did I ever tell you that Amrita had a huge crush on you?" I asked Aneesh as Amrita stared at me angrily and I winked at her.

Aneesh just laughed. "Last I remember, Meera told me she had it on you," he replied back.

"No seriously!" I continued. "She thinks you are the epitome of romance," I went on.

Amrita reprimanded me with, "Shut up, Palash,"even as her cheeks turned rosy.

"Who is Palash embarrassing now?" I heard Meera's voice behind me as she entered from the bedroom to the kitchen. I turned to look at a heavily pregnant Meera smiling at me from the doorway even as Aneesh stood up to help her in. I reached her before him.

"Oh my god! I am so happy for you," I said as I hugged her. And she replied with, "I know you are."

We both looked at each other for a while. "You colored your hair," she said and I smiled with tears in my eyes. I was genuinely happy for her and she knew that. I helped her to the chair.

"How did they allow you in the flight?" I had to ask.

She just shrugged. Aneesh placed the breakfast before her and she turned her nose up.

"You have to eat," he said

"I know but I don't feel like," she replied and then noticed Amrita. "I am sorry, I don't have an appetite, and you made so many things." She looked at the table.

"That's okay, you can tell me whatever you feel like eating. I will make it," Amrita offered and Meera's eyes lit up at that.

Aneesh noticed it. "Meera she is being a good host. Please don't unleash your inner hungry demon," he warned her.

"I really mean it," Amrita offered again.

"You asked for it then." Aneesh pointed at Amrita and then returned Meera's pleading glare with a smile asking her to go on.

"I want spicy curry, lasagna, Pav bhaji and lots of sweets," she announced.

"On it," Amrita replied and then I was sent out to buy the groceries.

Aneesh and Amrita were then in the kitchen preparing lunch for us as the non-cooks, Meera and I sat in front of the television.

"Thanks for having us, Palash," she said out of nowhere. I didn't reply but changed channels. We had a comfortable silence between us.

"Isn't this the stupid movie we both saw some years back?" she asked as I stopped at a channel.

I nodded. "Yeah you hated the climax."

"Oh yes. This is the one where the protagonist gets cancer at the end," she confirmed.

"Yeah, you thought that the director didn't know how to tie the loose ends because they got out of relationship," I reminded her.

"I remember," she replied, "and you believed that everyone needs closure. A story without closure wasn't saleable, hence the cancer."

I laughed as I remembered too. "Yes I said that."

"You still believe that, Palash?" she asked me and I looked up at her. She was sitting on the sofa with her legs on the table and I was sitting down on the carpet besides her with crossed legs.

"I don't know," I replied honestly. We could hear the laughter from the kitchen as Amrita and Aneesh joked about.

"Isn't this closure?" she asked next, and I shrugged.

"We moved on. We found the right marital partners for us who love us immensely and we still care for each other. We are all here for each other together. Isn't this closure?" she asked again rhetorically.

"Better than cancer," I replied and laughed.

"Better than cancer," she repeated as Aneesh came out with a plate of lasagna.

"This is the first course, madam," he said to her and placed the plate on her lap as he kissed her forehead and she murmured a thanks.

"He really loves you a lot," I said as he went back to the kitchen.

"So does Amrita," she replied.

"So, you decided to settle here?" I asked her next.

"Yes. My kids will need family around to grow up," she replied.

"Kids?" I asked surprised.

"They are twins. Both girls." She smiled at me and I could picture two little girls with Meera's features smiling.

"Give one to me," I said almost on autopilot and she laughed.

"Have your own."

"I don't think we are there yet," I replied

"I am surprised," she replied. "Your mother made my life hell in six months of marriage for an heir, how is she quiet now?"

"It's Amrita. No one dares to question her." It was true. My parents and Palak had met her once or twice in the past three years and just with her attitude she had conveyed to them that she was the one not to be messed with. Or maybe it was the previous experience with Meera but my family had finally given up on me. My mother called once a fortnight for about ten minutes and that was the only presence of her in my life whereas when I was with Meera she called daily for an hour and I entertained her. I was supposed to as she was my mother. Varun and I also met outdoors always. It was like my home was only a place for both of us. We never invited other people over, not even Amrita's friends. So, I was surprised when Amrita suggested to have Meera and Aneesh over. They were family for her.

"So, you are not having the talk of marriage too?" Meera asked next.

"I don't think of that, nor does she. If someday she does say she wants to get married we might. She is for now busy with her career and fed up of attending marriages of her clients I guess. She told me last time that she would have a court marriage. So yeah, when she says she is ready, we will walk to the court."

"And what do you want?" she asked me and I had to be honest with her.

"Frankly Meera, after you left I thought I was done with life. I wasn't even sure I was allowed to want things in life again. I have come a long way from that feeling. I felt useless like I wasn't even capable of holding on to a wife, like I was a big disappointment to the woman I loved. So, for now I am happy with things as they are. Amrita is incredible. I love her a lot and I think that's what I want. For things to stay as they are."

She nodded because she was the only person who understood what I just said.

"I am not giving you my kid," she said next and winked at me, eating the lasagna with bare hands.

"I will be the loving uncle then, who fulfills all their wishes that mummy daddy don't allow," I replied

"By all means," she said and so was it decided.

Amrita and Aneesh walked out with the rest of the meal that instance.

"Palash, you know Aneesh was telling me about the time you were drunk and you misbehaved at a party."

"And why was Aneesh telling you that?" I looked accusingly at Aneesh.

"Well, he was boasting that my boyfriend was still in love

with his wife." She winked at me.

"And what did you reply?" I asked her.

"What can I say?" she countered and I extended my hand to pull her to me. "You can tell him that your boyfriend will always care for his wife because she was his first love but right now right here is madly in love with you."

Amrita looked up at Aneesh and grinned. "Beat that, dude." As Aneesh sat beside Meera like nothing happened and started eating from her plate.

We were a family and in that instance, as I looked, I saw four happy people who understood each other and knew that they all were a pack, like the four suits.

I could see the flashy 'you won' that plays on the screen when you finish putting the decks together. I had won this game without the cancer. I had lost a wife and gained a family who genuinely cared for each other.

All the suits could start dancing on the screen now like it did at the end of the game.

This was closure.

THE END